A GRAVE CONJURING

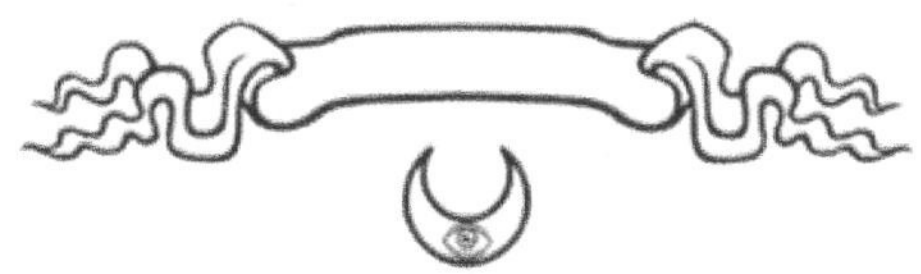

MICHELLE DOREY

The Haunted Ones 2

ISBN: 978-1-988913-09-4

Photo Images by Deposit Photos, used with permission
Edited by Paula Grundy
https://paulaproofreader.wixsite.com/home
Cover by Juan Padrone
https://www.juanjpadron.com/

Liane Blouin
849 Glenview Ave., Apt. 4
Wauwatosa, WI 53213

ONE

She actually paid money for this dump?" Ashley shook her head. Despite the fact that the heavy packing box made her arms ache, she couldn't help pausing a moment, taking in the cracked vinyl floor and the chipped paint on the cabinet doors. Her nose pinched, smelling the mustiness. The previous owner had been an old man, and he'd left that "old person" smell in the house. The heat in the stuffy kitchen wasn't helping either. "Yuck."

Maya nudged her shoulder, "Quiet. She's coming." She led the way across the room to the hallway and stopped, adjusting the bins in her arms before going up the stairs, "It's not that bad. At least with the lake, we'll have something to do this summer."

"How are you girls making out?" Aunt Claire came into the kitchen and dropped a box on the counter with a resounding bang. "That's the last of it for this trip." She smiled, wiping her hands on faded blue jeans. "Well? What do you think?"

Ashley forced a smile, "You weren't kidding when you said it was a fixer-upper. The setting is pretty nice though." Still, she couldn't help wondering if perhaps Aunt Claire had bitten off more than she could chew with *this* project. Sure, she had experience doing renovations but this one was beyond hope.

"That's why I bought it, doll! You won't recognize it once I'm done. Who knows? We may even stay here. I never thought I'd be able to afford a place on the lake. This might be my only chance." Taking a deep satisfied breath, Claire gazed out the window at the backyard sloping down to the water's edge.

Ashley turned, hiding her disappointment. Yeah, they were going to be stuck here for quite some time. She walked out of the room to join her sister at the top of the stairs. Each step higher tugged her gut lower. The house was in the middle of nowhere, a fifteen-minute walk to the nearest neighbor. If it were next year even, when she could get her driver's license, it might be bearable, but not now.

She trudged into the room at the far end of the hallway. It was only slightly bigger than Maya's room, but at least the view was better, overlooking the lake as opposed to the driveway. Setting the box on the bed, she couldn't help but notice the quietness in the air. When they'd lived downtown, there was always a car or people going past. Here, it was deathly still.

Footsteps sounded on the stairs, and a couple moments later, Aunt Claire stood in the doorway. "I'm heading back for another load at the old place. Do you want me to pick up pizza or hamburgers for lunch when I'm in town?"

Before she had a chance to answer, Maya popped out of her room. "Both! You're not thinking of cooking tonight, are you?" Her dark eyes shone while a wide grin flashed as she slipped by their aunt, stepping into Ashley's room.

"Good point." Aunt Claire laughed. "After this move, I'll be too tired to cook."

When Maya flashed a crooked smile, her milk chocolate eyes sparkled with mischief; it was a shot to Ashley's heart. Sometimes when Maya smiled and moved a certain way, it stunned her to see how much Maya resembled their mother. Of course she'd inherited the chestnut hair and lean athletic build, which was definitely all Mom. Ashley was their father's daughter, tall with his strawberry-blond hair, and the same shade as her aunt's.

Ashley sighed. Now wasn't the time to get melancholy, thinking of her parents. It was a little over two years that they'd been gone, thanks to that drunk driver. Still, moments of grief could sneak up and ambush you when you least expected it.

She shook it off, changing the subject, "Leah will be at the old house when you get back there, Aunt Claire. You're okay with giving her a ride out here?"

Her aunt nodded. "Of course. She can help you unpack and get your room organized. Carol's volunteered to give me a hand when she's done work."

Maya twirled a lock of hair around her finger, looking up at their aunt. "No Lucas? I thought he'd insist on helping you get settled."

The smile fell from Claire's lips. "He wanted to but I put him off. He'd be more in the way than anything. Carol will be a bigger help." She grinned. "Plus, it'll be fun having a girls' night! Something I haven't done in too long a time."

She glanced at her watch. "I'd better get going. You girls will be okay here on your own, won't you? Is there anything else you need me to pick up when I'm in town?"

Ashley shook her head slowly. This was it. This would probably be the way the summer would go—she and Maya alone while Aunt Claire was off selling houses. Alone and...

She hurried to the doorway and called to her aunt who was halfway down the stairs. "The internet. Can you call the company and ask them to put a rush on it?"

Claire looked up and shrugged. "I'll try, but it probably won't do any good. You might be stuck without TV or your laptops until Tuesday." Her eyebrows arched above a wide grin. "You may have to read or play board games. I remember playing Monopoly for hours when I was your age."

Maya raced forward and laughed, "You had to. Were computers even invented back then?"

Aunt Claire's eyes narrowed but the smile was still there, "Smart-ass. Yes, computers were around in 2005. I'm not that much older than you two! My parents weren't as indulgent with me. They actually set boundaries, if you can believe that."

"No way!"

"Totally! See you later. Call me if you think of anything you need me to pick up." Her footsteps were followed by the sound of the kitchen door closing.

Maya twirled on her heel and grinned. "Let's check out the outside. Maybe we can go for a swim before she gets back. I don't know about you but I'm melting. It's got to be almost ninety degrees in here."

Ashley blew at a lock of hair that lay plastered to her damp forehead. "Let's air this place out. We should have asked her to pick up more fans. How are we ever going to sleep without air-conditioning?"

She went over to the window and tugged on the lip of the frame. But it wasn't budging. "Give me a hand, will ya?"

Maya stood next to her, muttering as they strained to get the window to rise. "Probably the old guy who lived here never opened this window." It creaked and then rose up a few inches, refusing to go any higher. Her eyes flashed wide when she looked at Ashley. "You don't suppose he died in this house, do you?"

Ashley snorted. "Why? So what if he did? He had to die *somewhere*."

Maya was undeterred, her gaze darting around the room. "What if he's still here? I mean as a ghost or something, haunting the place?"

It wasn't a thought that Ashley wanted to dwell on. Plus, she was the oldest and therefore the responsible one. "That's just in horror movies. That kind of thing isn't real, Maya." But even so she couldn't resist. With fingers curled in front of her, Ashley pounced at her sister. "Boo!"

"Shut up!" Maya sniffed and held her head high walking out of the room. "I'm getting my bathing suit on and going for a swim. You can join me or stay here with the ghost. Your choice." She laughed and then sprinted down the hall.

Ashley chuckled as she pried the cardboard box open to

unpack. Maya was making the best of a bad situation. Her little sister was so much like her mother that it made her chest hurt. Mom had always seen the glass as half full, while Dad had been more pragmatic. It was time to be more like Maya and go with the flow.

Knowing Aunt Claire, they'd be moving again after a year or so. Nothing was forever. She knew that from experience.

TWO

Ten minutes later they stepped down the few rickety steps at the back door. Stalks of overgrown grass scraped her bare legs when Ashley made her way down the backyard to the dock. Like everything else about the property it was old with a few planks missing while the ones still there looked like they might collapse at any minute.

Her arm rose to stop Maya from going any farther. "Wait. Let me test it. If it holds me, then you'll be okay walking on it." She stepped gingerly on the first plank and when it didn't break she bounced a few times making sure it was safe before creeping slowly forward. The water on each side was shallow but dropped off at the end of the dock, judging by the deeper blue there.

"Hurry up, Ashley!" Maya huffed an exaggerated sigh before muttering, "I'm sure it's fine."

The board that Ashley tried next, gave way with a sharp crack. "Shit!" Her foot shot forward to the next plank, narrowly escaping a nasty fall. "See!" She glared back at her sister. "Maybe you should wade in from the shore. This thing's not too secure."

"Seriously? You're such a wimp!" Maya threw her towel down and then raced over the dock, her feet flying by the broken spots. She leapt from the end, curling her legs into her body for a perfect cannonball splash.

The dock wobbling under her feet from Maya's sprint destroyed Ashley's last attempt to balance. She toppled to the side, arms windmilling, falling into three feet of water. Her hips bumped against the sandy bottom near the dock, before she shook her head, spewing water and curses from her mouth. "You little jerk! I could have been killed. And you know better than to jump in like that! What if there was a rock or stump there?"

Maya ignored her, swimming farther out doing a smooth crawl stroke. Ashley gritted her teeth, and lunged forward trying to catch up. The little fool would probably swim to the other side of the lake if she didn't stop her. It was a good half mile across and while both of them could easily swim it, their aunt would be back soon. They were supposed to be unpacking.

"Wait up!" She slipped under the surface, pulling hard and kicking fast to join her sister. When she surfaced, gasping for air, there was no sign of Maya.

THREE

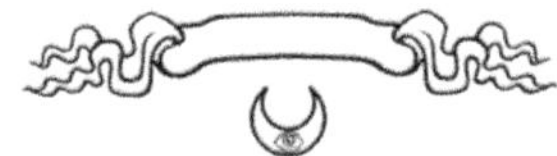

She tread water waiting for her to pop up. Where was she?

Something touched her foot and then closed over her ankle! Oh God, a weed or... The water closed over her head when she was yanked down. Kicking fast to escape, she peered through the murky darkness. Bubbles flitted by her face and then Maya was there, a smile plastered on her lips. Ashley scissored her legs fast, jettisoning up to the sun-kissed surface.

"You bitch! I'm gonna get you for that!" Ashley swam easily, following the froth of water that Maya churned up swimming back to shore.

"You'd have to catch me first!" Maya called over her shoulder.

With one strong kick of her legs Ashley shot forward and grabbed Maya's ankle. "Got ya!" She gave her a tug and her sister disappeared under the water.

Maya came up sputtering, "Okay! We're even!" She pulled away and tread water grinning at her sister. "This might not be too bad, y'know. Living here by the lake. We can get a canoe or even a small sailboat and learn how to sail. That could be fun."

"Yeah. Maybe." Ashley glanced over at the house and

thought of the boxes still sitting on the bedroom floor. "We should go back and finish the unpacking."

"Five more minutes! C'mon." Maya didn't wait for an answer but flipped sideways swimming out farther.

Ashley followed doing a lazy breaststroke, gazing at the far shore forested in deep shades of green. The sky was a clear, pristine blue and the sun cast sparking diamonds across the surface of the lake around her. The house might be a little isolated from their friends in town but at least she had Maya. And it was probably the last summer where the two of them could laze around together. She'd probably get a job the next year and wish for this time with Maya again.

"Hey! Wait up!" Ashley smiled swimming harder to catch up with her sister.

***

Ashley's stomach rumbled as she set the last hanger in the closet. She grabbed her phone from the dresser and checked the time. It was two hours since Aunt Claire had left and she should be back by now.

"She's here!" Maya let out a whoop and then her feet beat a fast tattoo down the stairs.

Ashley wasn't far behind, scooping her damp hair into a messy ponytail as she went. She passed by the bathroom where cardboard boxes formed a tower next to the vanity. Maybe Leah would help her cleaning the mess in there, so they could unpack and get that room squared away. But it was Leah's first time seeing the house. She'd definitely want a tour after lunch.

When she entered the kitchen, Leah was standing just inside the door gazing around at the cabinets to the far window overlooking the lake. She set the laundry hamper, filled with pots and pans on the counter and then looked over at Ashley. "This place is cool. I mean, it's old, yeah...but it's got lots of character." Her gaze flitted to Ashley's damp locks. "You've been swimming. Thanks for waiting."

"It was so hot upstairs we couldn't resist. Trust me, we'll be going again." Ashley went over to the table where her sister was tearing into the takeout bag of burgers. "Did you have lunch yet, Leah?" She grabbed one of the containers of fries and glanced over at her friend.

"I ate before I left home. You go ahead." Leah went over to the window next to them and gazed out at the yard and the lake. "My mom knew old Mr. Salter, the guy who owned this house. He went to the same church, at least until he got sick and died."

Maya swallowed fast and blurted, "Did he die here? Did your mother say anything about that?"

Before Leah had a chance to answer their Aunt Claire came in, loaded down with a bucket of cleaning supplies and the vacuum. "Save some for me girls." She set the things down and walked over to join them at the table, plucking a burger wrapped in foil, out of the bag. "That was the last load from the old house. We're officially living here now."

Leah flashed a grin at Claire. "I like this place. It's a little out of the way, but that's part of the charm." She turned to answer Maya. "Yeah. Mr. Salter died here. Mom said he went in his sleep, really peaceful. His son found him the next day."

Ashley sneaked a peek at Maya. Great. From the wide-eyed look of shock in her sister's eyes, she'd be thinking about this and would be jumping at her shadow. And of course Leah would feed into that as well. There wasn't a horror movie she hadn't seen. When it came to spooky, she ate it up like candy.

Leah glanced over at Ashley before adding quickly, "I don't think you need to worry, Maya. This place has a good feel to it. He was a nice, old guy."

Aunt Claire had been watching the exchange between Maya and Leah. She smiled and placed her hand on Maya's shoulder. "This place will be fine once we clean it up and decorate. You'll see. How was your swim?"

"Good. The dock needs some work. Ashley went through one of the boards."

Aunt Claire's gaze darted to Ashley. "You're okay, right? Maybe you two should stay off the dock until I can get around to fixing it." She finished the last bite of her burger and wiped her lips with a paper napkin. "I'm going to do some cleaning in here, give the cabinets a wipe. Even though it's the first room I'm renovating, that probably won't be for a few weeks." She rose and scooped up the empty bags and litter from the takeout meal.

Leah nudged Ashley. "I'm ready for the grand tour before we get to work." Her gray eyes lit up. "I love exploring old houses, seeing the odd nooks and crannies." Fishing a cell phone from her knapsack she added, "We should take some *before* pictures!"

"That reminds me..." Aunt Claire's smile fell when she looked at Ashley. "I spoke with the internet people. There were no openings before Tuesday."

"Thanks for trying, Aunt Claire."

"You've got your phone, so it's not as if you'll be cut off from the outside world." Leah led the way out of the kitchen and then stopped short in the small hallway. "Upstairs or down?"

Ashley shrugged. There wasn't anything all that interesting about the living room or dining room, just boxy rooms connected by an archway. "Upstairs. I'll show you my room."

When they walked up the stairs, Maya was right behind them. "Aunt Claire's got the biggest room of course, but I like my room. It's got built-in shelves and there's an entrance to the attic."

Leah turned, "Have you been up there to check it out? There might be some cool stuff hidden there. My grandmother's house is old like this, and she stores all kinds of neat shit in her attic. If Mr. Salter was anything like her, there might be stuff that his son overlooked."

Ashley rolled her eyes, "There might be lots of spiders too...or even bats and mice. Yuck." The thought of crawling around some dusty, old attic made her chest tighten. With her asthma, she was already wheezing a little just being in the main part of the house. She should have grabbed the vacuum and brought it up with her to give her room a good going over.

Maya spun on the newel post at the top of the stairs and

bounded across the hall to her room."You don't have to go up there. Leah and I will check it out."

"Hang on, Maya. I want to see this floor first." Leah peeked in the bathroom. "Nothing special here, although it needs some elbow grease."

Ashley nodded. "If you do the tub, I'll tackle the rest of it when we're ready." She continued down the hall on the other side of the stairs and stepped into her aunt's bedroom. Her bed and dresser were there along with packing boxes, almost totally covering the wooden floor.

Leah went in and wandered close to the window. "Wow! Nice view!"

"Yeah, my room's the same except it's half the size." Hearing Leah's praise took some of the sting out of living there. She'd get used to the house and maybe the exercise of riding the bike five miles into town would be good for her. For sure Maya wouldn't mind the ride.

"Leah! Come on!" Maya shouted from across the stairwell.

Leah grinned. "She's not the most patient person, is she?" With that she walked from the room to join her.

When Ashley got there, Maya held a broomstick aiming the hook on the end, through the eye bolt screwed on the ceiling door. Leah grabbed the stick and together the two of them tugged it open, jumping back quickly to avoid being hit by the ladder that slid to the floor. Particles of dust flitted through the air, released along with the old wooden access.

Covering her mouth and nose with her hand, Ashley peered up through the opening. Natural light from a window at the gabled end of the house revealed thick roof joists and curtains of cobwebs clinging to them.

"Cool!" Leah grabbed the sides of the ladder and began climbing. She paused at the top of the ladder looking around at the space.

"What's up there?" Maya was chomping at the bit to get up to the attic as well.

"There's an old trunk and a bunch of boxes." She scooped her cell phone out and flicked on the flashlight app. "You wouldn't like this place Ashley, not with your asthma. You were right about the spiders."

She aimed the flashlight around and then jerked back. "Shit! That scared the hell out of me!" She grinned looking down at Maya.

"What was it?" Maya's grip on the sides of the ladder loosened and she stepped back.

"It was an old mirror. My light flashed in the reflection, that's all. Come on!" Leah climbed the last few steps and then was gone.

Maya was wide-eyed looking over at Ashley. "I'm going. Are you?"

Ashley grabbed her inhaler from the pocket of her shorts and gulped a long blast of the Ventolin. It was probably the last place she should go but Maya was already climbing. Who knew what she could get into with Leah? If the floorboards up there were anything like the dock, she might go through and break her ankle.

Plus, Leah was acting kind of excited by whatever was up there, urging Maya to see it. She wouldn't mind checking it out either.

To be on the safe side, she rummaged in Maya's dresser for a scarf or shirt to filter the dust. She found a bandana and draped it over her nose and cheeks, tying it tight at the back of her head. She might look like a bandit but at least she wouldn't be inhaling so much dust. Slowly, she climbed the ancient rungs of the ladder, saying a silent prayer they wouldn't give out.

When she was eye level with the attic floor, she saw Leah and Maya kneeling beside some old wooden chest, rummaging around inside it. She glanced up at the cobwebs fluttering in the air from the commotion and the breeze funneling through the opening. If a spider came anywhere close to her, she would be out of there in a flash. All bets would be off, and Leah and Maya would be on their own.

She climbed the remaining rungs and then hunching to avoid touching anything above, she went over to join them.

"Awww..." Maya held up an old doll, draping the lace christening dress it wore over her bare arm. One blue eye of the doll's face was open while the other at an angle was almost shut completely. Maya adjusted the bonnet on its head as she gazed down at it. "It must have been one of their children's dolls. The Salter family, I mean."

"It's creepy, Maya. Put it down." Ashley mouth pursed tight staring at it. With the lines crisscrossing the plaster of the face, it was actually grotesque. She looked past her sister to what Leah had pulled out of the trunk.

Her friend held a school notebook thumbing through pages. Leah's lips pulled to the side. "Grade two, I'd guess." She tossed it back in the trunk and then grabbed a wooden truck with three wheels. "It's just old toys and kids' stuff. Maybe your aunt should contact the son in case he wants this crap."

Ashley edged closer and peeked inside the box, seeing some old clothes and more books and toys. "Yeah. This stuff might have some kind of sentimental value to him." She looked around and noticed the old mirror, which had startled Leah, propped up against a tower of boxes. She inhaled fast, trying to get oxygen into airways that were closing despite the inhaler. She'd have to get out of there soon before she had a full blown asthma attack.

Leah rose and then pried open a cardboard box next to the trunk. "Oh my..." She pulled a rectangular box from inside and held it up. "This is kind of weird to find up here. Especially for a churchgoing family."

Maya set the doll back in the trunk. "Why? Was is it? Some kind of game?" She brushed her hands together and then sat back on her haunches looking up at Leah.

"It's no game, Maya. This is a Ouija board." Leah could hardly keep the excitement from her voice as she hunkered down to the floor. Lifting the lid of the box off, she continued, "This thing's pretty old. These boards are used to summon the dead."

Ashley grit her teeth watching her sister's rapt attention on

Leah's words and the board. First the talk about old man Salter's ghost and now this. "Those things don't work, Maya. It's just superstition and a bunch of nonsense."

Leah shook her head. "That's not true. They do work. A girl in my Facebook group, Cindy, used one to contact her grandmother. The old lady told her things that only she would have known. And another guy, Allen, he—"

"How does it work?" Maya picked up a leaf-shaped object with a glass circle in the center. "What's this?"

Leah snatched it from Maya's hand. "It's called a planchette. This is the thing that spells out answers to questions people ask. It's not a game, Maya. It works."

Ashley forgot about her own discomfort and her rapid, shallow breathing. "It's bullshit is what it is, Maya. People make this thing move. They may not consciously be aware of it but they do. I read a story where a couple girls tried it. Right after the story was an explanation of how it worked."

"Just because you don't believe it, doesn't make it any less true, Ashley! That's just a theory. There's plenty of evidence that can't be explained away so easily." Leah set the board on the floor and unfolded it, showing an arc of letters of the alphabet on a golden-brown surface. A line of numbers, one to ten were above the word "Goodbye."

Maya's mouth was set tight when she peered at her sister. "What if it does work, Ashley? Wouldn't you like to be able to contact Mom or Dad? I know I would! Maybe we should try it."

Leah's gaze flitted from Maya to Ashley. It was obvious that her friend was on Maya's side. But of course she would be. If it was spooky, Leah was the self-appointed expert. She was even in some kooky, paranormal investigation Facebook group!

Ashley knew she'd have an adult ally in her logical-minded aunt. Claire wouldn't want Maya buying into this and scaring the living crap out of herself in the process. "We'll see what Aunt Claire thinks."

Leah shook her head. "You can't tell her. She'll take it away for sure. I wanted to buy a Ouija board a few years ago at Halloween, but my mom threw a fit! She said it was evil and wouldn't let me get it. Your aunt will probably be the same." Her eyes narrowed, challenging Ashley. "Besides which, if it doesn't work, why get all bent out of shape about it? You could at least try it once for Maya's sake."

Maya turned puppy-dog eyes at her sister. "What if we could talk to Mom and Dad? Don't you even want to try?"

FOUR

Ashley could feel her chest tighten even more looking at her sister. This time it had nothing to do with the dust in the air. Of course, she'd give anything to be able to talk to their parents. Her whole world had fallen apart that night when the police showed up at their door telling them about the accident. Aunt Claire had been staying with them at the time. She was back in town and licking her wounds from her marriage breakup. Thank God, she'd been there that night.

She gazed at the board. Her parents had died way too soon. She'd never had the chance to tell her mother how much she loved her, how much she appreciated all the things she'd sacrificed to raise them. And Dad...how many fathers took the time to teach their daughters things like riding a bike, swimming and how to throw a baseball? He'd helped with schoolwork but it would be the times outside in the fresh air learning sports that she'd always cherish most.

And Maya felt it too. And to make matters worse, Maya had been grounded for mouthing back to Mom on the night that their parents had died. She'd probably give her eye teeth to take back those words she'd flung at their mother before they left for their *date night.* Ashley could still hear Maya shouting how much she hated Mom and how she thought Mom was stupid. It didn't matter how many times Aunt Claire and she had tried to reassure Maya, that their parents knew Maya loved them. That memory would always haunt her sister.

"I won't tell Aunt Claire. Just don't be disappointed when you see it doesn't work, Maya." She scowled at Leah. "I've got to go down again. This place is killing me. Don't do anything with that board without me there." She'd talk to Leah later about this Ouija board, giving Maya some false hope of reaching their parents. If only it were that simple. But at least if she were there when they tried it, she'd keep Maya grounded, not buying into Leah's psychic nonsense.

She climbed down the ladder leaving them to rifle through the rest of the boxes for treasure. She tore the bandana from her face and reached for the inhaler. After a few deep breaths, she felt her breathing become deeper and slower.

When she went downstairs to get the vacuum and saw Aunt Claire straining to reach the top cabinet with the soapy sponge, she was tempted to let her in on what they'd found. But she'd given her word to Maya. Plus, her sister would tire of it when she saw it didn't work. Best to leave the subject of the Ouija board alone. Her aunt had more than her hands full without dealing with some bullshit board game as well.

"What time is Carol coming out to give you a hand? Do you need my help in here?" Ashley steadied the chair that Claire stood on when she rose to her tiptoes to get the back of the shelf in the cabinet. The woman was a workhorse when she set her mind to a project. And this house was definitely a project.

Claire lowered and then tossed the sponge onto the counter. She wiped her hand across her forehead and smiled. "I'm good. Carol will be here in a couple of hours. How's it going upstairs?"

Ashley shrugged. "It's dusty but my room is getting there. We'll clean the bathroom and then go over everything with the vacuum. I'm going for a swim after that. You should take a break and join us."

Claire stepped down from the chair and put her hand on Ashley's shoulder. "I might just do that, Ash. It's too hot to keep this pace up. It's pretty quiet upstairs. Are Leah and Maya helping or goofing off?"

"Don't worry. I'm about to read the riot act to Maya. She was showing Leah her room when I came down." She was about to leave the kitchen but Claire held her arm.

"How's your breathing, doll? You doing okay in all this dust?" Her eyes narrowed examining Ashley's face.

Ashley patted the pocket where her inhaler was. "I've had to use the puffer a few times, but I'll be fine once the dust is cleaned up."

Aunt Claire's eyebrows arched, "I probably should have hired someone to do this cleaning before you got here. Just take it easy and get Maya to do the vacuuming, okay?"

"Sure." Ashley strained maneuvering the vacuum out of the kitchen and then up the stairs. They'd better be finished in that dirty old attic or she was gonna strangle them. She set the machine down with a thud just outside Maya's bedroom doorway.

Maya stood on the bottom rung of the ladder reaching for the board that Leah extended from the space above. She held it in her hands looking at the childish scribbles and a drawing of a spooky face written in red marker on the cover. She glanced at Ashley. "Who's C. V., I wonder? Wasn't their last name Salter?"

Ashley rolled her eyes and sighed. "Who knows? You'd better put that thing away and do the vacuuming."

Leah stepped down and brushed the dirt from her hands on her jean shorts. "Yeah. We'll try it out tonight, Maya. It's better when we create the right atmosphere and it's quiet. In the meantime, put it in your dresser out of sight, in case your aunt comes in."

Maya's eyes glistened when she looked over at her sister. "I really hope we can get some kind of message to Mom and Dad."

Ashley felt her heart ache seeing the sadness in her sister's face. Maybe if Maya used the board and thought she was contacting their mother it would ease her guilt. Would it hurt if the planchette *helped* to accomplish that? There might be some good that could come of it, even if it was a hoax.

Leah took the board and opening the bottom drawer of Maya's dresser, she slid it inside carefully like she was holding something sacred. "We'll try, Maya. If it doesn't work the first time, we'll keep doing it until you reach them."

Maya blinked a few times and then gave her head a little shake, forcing a smile. "Kind of like getting a busy signal? So we keep calling, leaving messages? Is that it?"

Although Ashley snorted, she was glad that her twelve-year-old, smart-ass, pain-in-the-butt sister was back again. "It's call-waiting in another dimension." She laughed and then pointed to the vacuum. "The sooner we get this work done, the faster we'll get outside to go swimming again. C'mon, Leah. There are rubber gloves with our names on them."

Leah followed Ashley from the room. "You guys won't be laughing tonight when we contact the spirit world. But yeah, for now I'd like to get this work done and jump in the lake."

Ten minutes later with the drone of the vacuum filling the upstairs, Ashley paused from scrubbing the bathroom sink. She turned to Leah who was on her knees bent over and wiping down the bathtub. "You know Maya had a fight with Mom the night my parents were killed, don't you?"

Leah's lower lip extended blowing a stray lock of dirty-blond hair from her nose. "Yeah. You told me. The poor kid. I can't imagine how awful she must feel about that."

Ashley nodded but inside she was replaying that horrible night for like the hundredth time. "Yeah. You know I don't believe in any of this. But if you were to kind of direct that planchette thing like it was my mom forgiving Maya and telling her she was loved, it wouldn't be a bad thing for her to see."

Leah sat back on her haunches and sighed. "That won't be necessary, but I get your point, Ashley. If you had read even half as much about this stuff as I have, you'd see. There are so many in this group I belong to...people who've had seriously spooky things, messages, and signs that have happened to them, that you can't dismiss it. I'm sure some of it is BS but not for the bulk of it, not from what people have written."

"Leah..." Oh no. She was off on a tangent that would be hard to stop. She looked into Leah's eyes and felt her body sink lower. Now she was gonna talk about pyramids, crystals, and all that other crap. She'd heard it all before but that wouldn't stop Leah.

Leah leaned closer and even though the vacuum was still buzzing keeping Maya busy, her voice was lower, "Just keep an open mind, will ya? It won't help having a skeptic like you present when we do this. If you won't do it for me, then do it for your sister. Okay?"

Ashley had dodged a bullet, just barely. She shrugged. "Sure. I'll try. For Maya."

She didn't want to admit it, but a kernel of hope niggled in her gut that maybe this thing would work. "How'd you find this group, Leah?"

Leah laughed. "Are you serious? There's a Facebook group for *everything*! There are people from Europe, Australia, practically everywhere, but mostly it's the U.S. I'll send you an invite to join if you want."

"No. I'm good." Ashley continued with cleaning the vanity. "So, your mom is freaked out about this?"

"Totally. She quoted chapter and verse from the Bible about consorting with demons." Leah paused for a moment. "But from what I've learned she isn't totally out to lunch on that. There's a protocol with these boards. You always, *always* say "goodbye" when you end a session. Apparently you leave a portal open if you don't do that. Not all spirits on the other side are nice. Some are demonic."

"Riiight." Ashley dismissed Leah's words, standing up and looking around. The air smelled like pine from the cleaning solution and everything shone from their efforts. She set the rags in the bucket and then smiled at Leah. "Aunt Claire has her hands full with the downstairs. I think I'll make her bed and try to get her room organized."

"I'll help you. And then let's get changed. I can't get in that lake fast enough."

Leah pulled the door open wider and then slipped out just as Maya turned the vacuum off. The stillness of the house hit her like a hammer. No cars outside or people chatting as they strolled by on the sidewalk.

They really were in the middle of nowhere.

FIVE

"You guys are finished? I think you gave me the hardest job." Maya pulled a face and then dragged the vacuum down the hall to their aunt's room. Looking around, she sighed, "Are you kidding? I can't do this room until the boxes are gone."

Ashley stepped by her, entering Claire's bedroom. "Help us sort things out and make a path at least."

Leah was busy tearing the lid from the first box she found. She held up a white photo album with a picture of a pair of lovebirds holding a pink ribbon in their beaks—the ends forming a heart. "Your aunt's wedding pictures?"

Ashley's brow furrowed. In the two years they'd been with Claire, she'd never seen this album. As far as she knew, Claire and Jake had eloped and got married in Las Vegas. There were actually pictures that she'd squirreled away?

She took the book from Leah and leafed through it while Leah and Maya were like vultures peering over her shoulder at the photos. The first one was of the two of them together, Claire in a pale blue satin dress that was a perfect complement to the upsweep of strawberry- blond hair. Her eyes were laughing and bright as she snuggled close to Jake.

Leah leaned so close she could feel her breath on her shoulder. "Wow. He's hot. Look at those eyes. Whatever happened that they broke up? He's so much better looking than Lucas."

Ashley gazed at the picture, remembering a visit with her aunt and Jake one Fourth of July weekend. He'd been fun, always joking around and as a couple they'd seemed so good together. He'd bought Ashley and Maya ice cream and taken them on the ferris wheel at the amusement park set up for the holiday. Her aunt and Jake had lived six hours away and didn't get to town often, so the visit had been memorable.

Maya's finger dawdled on one of the wedding photos as she spoke. "Yeah, he was so much nicer than Lucas. I swear that guy hates us. Sometimes I catch him looking at us when Aunt Claire is in the other room. It's like he resents the fact that we're here." Maya looked up at her sister for confirmation.

Ashley's eyebrows rose but she held her tongue. She'd gotten the same vibe from Lucas, but it wouldn't do to encourage Maya in this train of thought. So far, Claire had resisted his attempts to move in together. She'd overheard her aunt one night telling Lucas she needed her own space for a while.

She shut the book and then set it on Claire's dresser. "We probably shouldn't be looking at these photos. I mean she never brought the album out so maybe there's private stuff in there."

Leah laughed and made a leap to grab the book. "All the more reason to look! Maybe there's 'honeymoon' candid shots if you know what I mean."

Ashley grabbed her arm before she could get it.

Leah shook her head. "I'm kidding. You're right. If she wanted us to see them, she'd show us. But that ex is gorgeous."

"I wish she were still with him." Maya set about unpacking the rest of the box. She tossed a set of sheets and pillowcases onto the bed. "Let's get this over with and get outside."

Forty minutes later they were changed into their bathing

suits, with towels draped over their arms, clomping down the stairs. Ashley stopped at the kitchen door and saw their aunt wringing out a cloth and setting it over the tap. The scent of ammonia mingled with the tangy smell of pine from all her hard work. "We're pretty well done upstairs. You coming swimming with us?"

"Absolutely! You three go ahead and I'll be out in a few minutes to join you." Aunt Claire dried her hands on a towel and then looked around at the kitchen. "I can see us spending most of our time in here. I love a big country kitchen, don't you?"

Ashley looked around trying to imagine how it might look with updated cabinets and new flooring. Yeah. It could be nice. "You did a good job in here. And if I know you, it'll be like something out of a decorating magazine by the time you're finished. It's nice." For the first time, she actually felt like she meant it.

"Thanks. I really hope you like it. It's going to be home for you for a few more years. At least until you go off to college. I know it's off the beaten track, but next year you'll have your driver's license and it won't seem so remote." Claire's hand rested on the counter as she stood looking at them. For a moment there was sadness in her eyes as well as love. "We're a team, girls. Unbeatable."

Maya walked down the short hall calling over her shoulder, "Come on! Last one in's a rotten egg!"

"Wade in! Stay off that dock, Maya!" Claire sprinted forward but the only thing to see was the screen door banging shut and a flash of Maya racing to the water.

Ashley grinned. "I'll keep an eye on her. Don't worry."

Leah was the next one flying through the door with Ashley on her heels. She tossed the towel onto the grass and was stepping into the cool water when a shout behind her made her turn.

"Leah! Ashley!"

She shielded her eyes from the glare of the sun and peered at the two boys leaning their bikes against the tree at the side of the drive. It was Leah's younger brother, Preston and his friend, Henry. What the hell?

"Does Mom know you're here?" Leah stood in the water up to her waist glaring at Preston. She shot a look at Ashley and muttered, "He's only here because of Maya."

Ashley smiled and looked out to where her sister was floating on her back oblivious to everything. Poor Preston. He had it bad for Maya, but Henry was the one Maya liked. A total smart-ass "cut from the same cloth" as her mother used to say.

Preston waved his hand over his head. "She kn...knows!"

That was another thing in Henry's favor. Preston had been to speech therapists but none seemed able to fix his stutter.

Henry made a leer. "Why, Leah? You want to spend some time just with meee?"

Leah scoffed. "In your dreams, junior." She took a swing at him.

With an evil cackle, he skittered out of range and down to the lake. Henry peeled his shirt off and ran past Ashley. He was also taller than Preston and there was always a smirky grin on his face. "Hey Mayan! How's the water?" But he didn't wait for her answer, racing in up to his thighs and then swimming like an eel.

"Wa...wait for muh...me!" Preston's shirt flew through the air and he toed his sneakers off. He made his way across the grass, his tender feet jerking high with every step. To make matters worse, when he spoke half the time his voice modulated between the deeper teenage one to an adolescent squeak.

"That Henry's such a jerk, always with the wiseass cracks." Leah folded her arms. "Except for Preston. He's never, not once, ever made fun of Preston's speech impediment." She snorted. "He's still a jerk though."

Ashley laughed sneaking a look at Leah. "So much for peace and quiet with these two." She walked in farther feeling the sandy bottom squishing between her toes. The water was cool on her skin, while above the July sun baked her shoulders. She sank down and joined Leah, swimming out to join Maya and the boys.

When the screen door banged shut, she turned and saw her aunt walking across the yard. She had pulled her hair up into a ponytail and with the dark sunglasses and tankini she could have passed for their older sister.

"Hey guys!" She flashed a smile and tossed the glasses and towel onto the grass. "How's the water?" She peered out past the dock watching Maya and the guys.

"Great! You know what you need Ms. Vincent? A raft! We could help you make one." Henry flashed a smile watching Claire.

Claire waded in, looking at the dock where Ashley had gone through. "First of all, it's Claire. 'Ms. Vincent' was my mother. And if you guys want to take that project on, I'll buy the wood and barrels. Knock yourself out."

Ashley caught up to Preston who was waiting for a chance to speak to Maya, watching her try to duck Henry under the water. "Hey Preston. I'm glad you guys came out for a swim. How long did it take you to ride out?"

Preston turned his round face to look at her. He had the same complexion as Leah, kind of pale with a smattering of freckles across his nose and the same gray eyes. Even his hair was the same shade of dishwater blond falling over his forehead into his eyes. "Twe...twenty meh...minutes. Nuh...not too bad."

"Yeah. That's not too bad. But it's kind of downhill, right? I'm sure it'll take me and Maya longer to go into town." She tread water and tried to ignore Maya laughing at something Henry said.

Aunt Claire swam past them, calling over her shoulder to Preston, "You guys are welcome to stay for dinner if you'd like. That's if you clear it with your parents."

Even though it seemed like Henry and Maya were clowning around in a world of their own, Maya chimed in, "Yeah! Why don't you and Preston stay? We could even build a campfire and toast marshmallows." She flashed a smile at Preston. "It only took you twenty minutes to ride out. It doesn't get dark till almost nine."

It was Leah who answered, "I'm not sure Mom would want you riding back in the evening. You'd better check with her, Pres."

Henry spoke, "No problem with a ride back! My brother is off work at seven. He can come pick us up and put our bikes in the back of the truck. He won't mind."

Leah's head tipped to the side. "Your brother? Is he back in town? I thought he was living with your dad in Wilmington."

Ashley's ears perked up too. Henry's brother, Mason, had been the heartthrob of Saranac High before he left a year ago to try living with his father. Her gaze darted to Leah, both of them on the same page. *Mason Sherwood* was back! And he might be coming out later to pick up his brother. Yowza.

"He wanted to come back for the summer. And when he got the job at the gas station it sealed the deal." Henry bobbed under and when he came up he shot a jet of water from his cheeks at Maya.

"Hey! Duh...Don't do th...that!" Preston pushed through the water and his hands gripped Henry's shoulders, dunking him. He glanced over at Maya and his cheeks flushed. "He's dis...disgusting sometimes."

He barely got the words out when he disappeared under the surface and Henry's head bobbed high. Maya laughed and then dove under.

Leah sighed. "They're such jerks. Honestly." She smiled at Ashley, both of them doing a lazy crawl swimming out to join Claire. "I'm glad I brought makeup. I almost didn't. Mason Sherwood. Maybe we can talk him into staying for a while."

Ashley snickered. "Roasting marshmallows, right?"

"Something like that."

SIX

Ashley and Leah treaded water when they reached Claire who was stretched out floating lazily. The others were closer to shore, still having noisy fun trying to elude each other in some kind of dive and dunk game.

Claire's head rose and she smiled at Ashley. "I guess I'd better go in and try to catch Carol before she comes out. Pizza isn't going to cut it with these guys staying for dinner."

"Maybe ask her to pick up some hotdogs." Ashley looked over to where her sister let out a sharp yelp before disappearing under the water. "We thought we could have campfire. That's okay right?"

Her aunt nodded. "Sure. If you guys want to gather some rocks and set that up, it's fine by me. Just don't put it too close to the house." She started back for shore in an easy side stroke. "Actually, I'd better pick the spot. I'll set a lawn chair where I think you should build it. Then I'll call Carol. How's that?"

Leah answered for both of them, "That's great! Thanks for asking my brother and Henry for dinner. That was nice of you."

Claire's smile went wider. "Nice for you girls too! I heard

that a certain someone is back in town to give the guys a lift home. That wouldn't have anything to do with the sudden interest in a campfire, would it?"

Ashley felt her cheeks grow hotter but she grinned. "Busted. Aunt Claire, even you have to admit he's cute."

Leah flicked some water droplets at her. "Cute! That's like saying the Biebs is just a...well, you know what I mean. Come to think of it, Mason kind of looks like Justin Bieber."

"Whatever." Claire laughed, swimming harder to get to shore.

Leah looked over at Ashley. "You just about done with swimming? I know I am."

Ashley's eyes twinkled. "You need time to dry and style your hair, put makeup on and do your nails. I get it."

Leah splashed more water at Ashley and laughed. "Look who's talking!" She pushed herself forward scissoring her legs. "Race ya!"

But Ashley wasn't even going to try. She swam over to where Maya was. "You guys want to make a fire pit? You can use some of the rocks on the shore."

Preston was the first to answer, "Shu...sure! C'mon Henry. It wuh...won't take lah...long if we all duh...do it." He flashed a smile at Maya and then started swimming to the shore.

"C'mon Mayan. Let's go!" Henry dipped under and when he surfaced he was alongside Preston.

Ashley couldn't help herself. "Yeah Mayan. Hop to it."

Maya rolled her eyes and took off after the two boys.

Ashley took her time swimming in to shore. She gazed at the rust-colored brick of the house and the tall pines with sweeping boughs bordering it like sentinels. It actually was very pretty when you saw it from the lake. Even the forests bordering the property with a backdrop of high hills in the distance was picturesque like a postcard.

On the edge of the lake, Maya and her friends hopped from rock to rock bantering as they picked rocks while Leah stood next to the lawn chair drying her hair with the towel. The house may be out of the way but not so far that their friends couldn't visit. Having them there the first day might be a harbinger of good days ahead. The move was turning out way better than her first impression.

Her feet touched bottom and she stood up, squeezing water from the long locks of her hair. She wandered over to Leah just as the other three arrived carrying round stones.

Maya looked over at Henry. "Guess what we found in the attic earlier."

Ashley shot a look at Leah. Shit. Maya was going to blab about the Ouija board in front of Preston. Leah would catch hell for sure if he told their mother. "Maya!" She signaled with her eyes for Maya to stop, her gaze flitting to Preston.

But Henry didn't catch it as he was positioning a rock. "What? A dead body? Some bats? What did you find?"

Maya had picked up on the message and she mumbled, "Just some old toys in a trunk. Not that fascinating really."

Preston nudged her with his shoulder. "Thuh...that sounds cool. I...I'd like to see." His cheeks kind of flushed as he watched her. "Muh...maybe some of it's va...valuable. Like in Aaa...*Antique Roadshow*."

Ashley answered, "It's just a bunch of junk and tons of dust. Nothing cool about it."

"Yeah. I wouldn't mind checking it out." Henry rose to his feet. "Maybe after we get this pit squared away, okay? Preston's right. Some of the things those guys find in people's attics are worth thousands of dollars. Who knows? You could be thousand-aires."

The screen door opened and Claire stood in the opening leaning out. "Anyone want a soda? Did you guys call home to let your parents know you're staying for dinner?"

Maya looked at both guys and hissed, "Don't tell Aunt Claire we were in the attic, okay?"

Henry looked puzzled for a moment before he shouted over to Claire, "If you have coke that would be great! I'm going to call home right now. Thanks for reminding me."

"Yuh...yeah. A coke pluh...please." Preston grabbed his shirt from the lawn where he'd dropped it. He took his cell phone out and then turned his back to make the call home.

When Claire went back inside to get their drinks, Henry spun on Maya. "Why don't you want your aunt to know about the attic? What's up with that?"

Maya scowled at her sister and then blurted it out, "We found a Ouija board. We're going to try it later but Leah thinks Aunt Claire will be pissed if we do."

Henry's head tipped. "Why? From what I know about those things, they don't work, so what's the big deal?"

Leah had heard enough. "Says who? My mom must believe in them because she had a shit fit when I wanted to buy one."

Maya joined in, "Look, we want to try it to see if we can connect to my parents, okay?"

Henry pulled back and his mouth snapped shut, while Preston turned around to join in, "Whu...what are you gu...guys talking about?"

"It's a secret." But it was clear that Maya wanted to tell him. "You can't tell anyone...especially your mother."

Ashley looked over at Leah. She looked like she was ready to throttle Maya.

"I wuh...won't tell. What is it?" His gaze flitted from Henry to Maya.

"We found a Ouija board and we're going to try it later tonight. But you can't tell anyone, k?" Maya leaned into him.

"Shu...sure." His eyes were puzzled when he looked over at Leah. "Thu...that's weird that o...old man Salter had a Ouija buh...board."

She shrugged. "Maybe his kids owned it. I mean the attic has lots of their toys."

Henry spoke to Maya, "So how are we going to manage this without your aunt coming in and catching us?"

"I don't know. Maybe she'll be busy talking to Carol. We can pretend we're playing cards or Monopoly maybe. We'll figure something out, and if not, you guys will just have to wait and hear about it tomorrow." Maya peered at Leah and Ashley. "The three of us can do it when Aunt Claire goes to bed."

Ashley folded her arms across her chest. "That was the

original plan, Maya. You're the one who blabbed to everyone." She still wasn't sure about any of this but if Preston said anything, there would be hell to pay at Leah's house. Maybe her mother wouldn't be so keen on Leah coming out to visit if she knew.

Leah stepped closer to her brother and scowled at him, "If you do this with us, you can't tell Mom or else you're telling on yourself too."

Ashley nodded. Leah had a point. She turned to Maya and the boys. "Can you guys handle finishing the fire pit? Leah and I are going in to get changed."

As they walked across the lawn, Carol's jeep pulled into the driveway behind their aunt's car. She got out, carrying groceries and wine, yelling over a friendly, "hi."

Ashley waved before turning to whisper to Leah, "I think we'll be able to do the silly Ouija board with your brother and Henry. I think Aunt Claire and Carol are going to have a few drinks and catch up. She said earlier that she was looking forward to a girls' night."

Leah nodded. "Actually, it might work better with more people. Even Preston will be a help and then he can't rat us out." She laughed and held the door for Ashley.

When they went inside, Carol was getting the tour of the kitchen while Claire described all the changes she had planned.

Ashley passed them as they were coming out. "We're going to get changed. Maya and the guys are making some headway with the fire pit." She smiled at Carol. "Did you bring your bathing suit? The water's great!"

Carol's hand rose like a traffic cop's. "I'm not a big fan of swimming in lakes. Give me a pool at the Four Seasons and I'm good! Girl, I need to see my toes, not get them nibbled on by some fish." She flashed a grin with brilliant white teeth against her smooth coffee-toned skin. Her dark eyes were lit with fun so it was impossible not to grin right back.

Aunt Claire laughed. "After you've have some wine, you may change your mind, Carol. I might go in again too. That's the plus of being here. Might as well enjoy it."

"Speaking of which...if the upstairs is off-limits with the girls changing, we might as well christen the house with some wine. C'mon Claire. You've been working all day." Carol grabbed Claire's arm and tugged her back into the kitchen.

Claire chuckled. "So have you! How much money did the casino make today? You really should skim a little cream off, go on that vacation you've always wanted. You do the books, so they'd never know."

"Yeah right! And *my* new home would be prison. No thanks."

Ashley turned to Leah. "You take the bathroom and I'll change in my room. Just don't take hours, okay? Mason may not even get out of his truck when he picks up Henry."

Leah raced ahead. "I'm not taking any chances." She turned and smiled at Ashley. "Just don't hate me when he asks me out."

Ashley rolled her eyes. "What if he asks *me* out?"

"I will definitely hate you." She laughed and continued up the stairs.

SEVEN

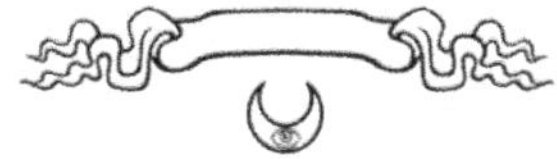

The sun was a fiery ball on the horizon, streaking the sky above the lake with ribbons of orange, red, and pink by the time that Ashley and Leah joined the gang at the fire pit.

Carol looked up from her place next to the crackling fire and grinned at Ashley. "Ooo eee! Something smells really nice! Is that Dior or Faberge?"

Ashley could feel her cheeks warm when every set of eyes were focused on her. "Neither. It's just body wash."

Leah plopped down in an empty lawn chair. "Japanese Cherry Blossom. It's nice, isn't it. I've got to get Mom to buy me some. I love it." She looked over at Preston, "You should get changed out of that damp swimsuit. Did you bring a change of clothes?"

Maya stood up, "You two were hogging the upstairs, so no one got a chance. We're all dry now anyway. But I'm done with swimming, so I'm putting on my sweats." She turned to Henry. "If you and Preston want to change, I'll show you where the bathroom is. Actually, you haven't seen the house at all."

Henry threw one last branch from the bundle next to the

fire and then got up. "Sure." He turned to Preston, "Let's go, bud."

Preston wasted no time racing over to where they'd dumped their bikes, grabbing both knapsacks. "Wuh...wait for me." He hurried over to the back door and followed them in.

Aunt Claire looked over at Carol, "I suppose we should bring the food out. I need another top up of wine anyway."

"You don't have to ask *me* twice." She rose and then directed her next words at the girls, "How about you get a table and bring it out for the food? That is, if you can take a chance on not wrecking your manicure. I've got to see this guy that's got you two all dolled up. Maybe I'll make a play for him myself."

Ashley primped her hair with her hand, doing her best vamp. "This old thing? We always look good, and Mason is way too young for you, Carol."

Carol let out a whoop. "Ever hear the term *Cougar*, girls?" She laughed, following Claire into the house.

"Cougar? Oh my God." Leah snickered as she rose, "We'd better give them a hand. Seriously, do we look that obvious?"

"Probably." Ashley nodded to the side signaling to go, "I think there's an old card table we can use. It's in the laundry room. I saw it when I put our bathing suits in the dryer."

When they went inside, Claire was loading a tray with wieners, buns, and condiments while Carol topped up their glasses with fresh wine. Ashley halted before going down the hallway to the laundry room. "You're staying the night aren't you, Carol?"

Carol nodded and her face was serious looking over. "Of course, Ashley. My sleeping bag's in the jeep. I knew we'd be drinking and gossiping till all hours. Especially since I don't work tomorrow."

Ashley felt her chest loosen. After what she'd been through—her parents killed by a drunk driver—she had zero tolerance for that. "Good. We can make pancakes tomorrow morning. It'll be fun."

Leah piped up, "After supper maybe we'll play some cards

or a game with Maya and the guys. We'll try to stay out of your hair. Just don't gossip about us, okay?"

Ashley's eyes met Leah's. She was setting this up already, time alone with that Ouija board. Part of her felt a little guilty about it, sneaking around but another part had her wondering. It was probably silly but what if...

Aunt Claire took the glass of wine from Carol and had a sip. "That's really hitting the spot."

Ashley smiled and followed Leah into the laundry room. Aunt Claire was having a good time with Carol and was fine with their plans. Her voice was low when she spoke, "How long does this take...this Ouija board thing?"

Leah shrugged. "It depends I guess." When Ashley shot her a puzzled look, she continued, "If there's any spirit out there who wants to connect it could be fast or maybe it'll take longer. I don't know for sure."

"What time will your mom be expecting Preston home? I mean, how much time do we have for this?"

"You're *really* wondering about Mason...whether we'll be still doing the Ouija board when he arrives and you don't get to see him. That's it, isn't it?" Leah's eyes glinted. "Don't worry. I want to see him too."

They went into the laundry room and Ashley threaded her way through a few boxes to grab the card table.

***

It was just about dark when they finished eating. The campfire had burned low, but Claire and Carol seemed content to just sit gazing into the flames, drinking wine.

Maya stood up. "Who's up for some cards or a game of Monopoly?"

Aunt Claire looked at her watch. "What time is your brother coming, Henry? You might not have time for Monopoly...or as we used to call it, Monotony. That game goes on for hours."

Preston stood up to join Maya. "Ye...yeah. How about gi...gin rummy instead?"

Henry looked at Aunt Claire. "He said he'll be here at nine. Just a bit over an hour. Enough time for me to whup everyone's butt in a game of gin rummy."

Getting up as well, Leah chimed in, "You're looking at the world's champ in that game, my friend." She picked up the condiments and piled everything onto the tray. "We'll get this, Claire. You ladies just enjoy the fire and relax."

Ashley grabbed the rest of the stuff and followed the others into the house. Maya and the two boys raced ahead of her and Leah, their feet pounding on the stairs like a herd of elephants. They set the things on the counter and weren't long after them.

Leah entered Maya's bedroom and got the board out of the bottom drawer. She looked around the room. "We should have the lights low and some candles but this will have to do I guess. What about if your aunt—"

"I'm ahead of you." Maya held up a deck of playing cards. "If we hear her, we'll stop and deal the cards."

"I think she's pretty comfortable where she is." Henry laughed and then when Leah squatted down in the middle of the floor setting the board up, he lowered too.

Maya grabbed the bandana that Ashley has used earlier and draped it over her bedside lamp. She stepped over to the doorway and flipped the overhead light off. The room was now dim, lit only by the reddish hue of the bedside light. "How's that?"

"Good." Leah looked around at each of them. "The thing is, no matter if Claire's coming upstairs, we have to close off communication the correct way. We have to move the planchette to "Goodbye". Got that? It's *super* important."

Each of them nodded, but their eyes were riveted to the board. Even Ashley felt a chill in Leah's warning. The dimmer lighting in the room helped as well.

Leah put the planchette in the middle of the board. "Everyone put the fingers of your left hand lightly on the reader." She demonstrated by placing the tips of her fingers there.

Ashley took a deep breath and moved her hand over, barely

touching the small wooden object.

When they were all positioned, Leah continued, "Are there any spirits present?"

The planchette remained in the middle of the board. Ashley couldn't help looking at her sister who was across from her, next to Leah. Maya's gaze roamed over the room as if searching for some sign.

"We ask again, are there benign spirits here who wish to communicate with us?"

When again nothing happened, Henry piped up, "C'mon. We don't have all day, here."

"Shush!" Maya shot a dark look at him.

Ashley noticed the corners of Henry's mouth twitch trying to keep from laughing while Preston was staring intently at the little planchette. She was more in line with Henry's train of thought.

Leah cleared her throat and spoke again, "We wish to communicate with Maya and Ashley's parents. Robert or Gail, are you here? Your daughters wish to contact you."

Everything was still for a few minutes. Ashley could hear their breathing, feel a little tremble from their fingers on the leaf-shaped object. But nothing was happening.

"Gail Vincent, Maya would like to talk to you. Please come to us if you can." Leah wasn't giving up.

The planchette moved slightly and Ashley looked over at her sister. Maya's eyes were as big as marbles staring at the planchette. She glanced at Leah only to find her peering at the word "Yes". Had she moved it in that direction?

"Are you with us, Gail? Please give us a sign that it is you we are communicating with."

The planchette continued inching slowly across the board to the word "Yes."

Ashley's gaze flitted to Leah and Maya. Leah could be making the planchette move for Maya's sake. The movement had been slow and deliberate like she was forcing it.

Henry sighed. "Who's pushing this thing? Seriously?" He took his hand away and then folded his arms across his chest.

"This is bogus, guys."

Maya glared at him. "Shut up, Henry."

Preston added his two cents to his friend's skepticism, "Ye...yeah Henry. Ju...just because yu...you don't believe doesn't mean ih...it's not wu...working. Be quiet."

Henry's eyes narrowed. "Test it then. If you think it's really Maya's mother, ask it a question only Maya knows the answer to. We'll see if it moves then."

All eyes turned to Maya waiting for her to speak. Finally she did. "What did I call my first teddy bear?"

But Henry wasn't buying it. "Ashley probably knows the answer to that. Try something only you and your mother shared."

This time it was even longer waiting for Maya to think of a question. All the while Ashley deliberated whether she should take her hand away, let it play out naturally to see if there might be a grain of truth to the board.

"Okay." Maya glanced at Ashley. "I don't think you know this one, but tell me if you do, k? Where did my mother take me after my first trip to the dentist?"

Ashley shook her head. "I was in school that day. I kind of remember you going but it was just you and Mom. I don't know."

Leah looked at Maya. "Go ahead. You ask the question this time."

Maya shot a look at Ashley and then spoke, "Where did you take me after the dentist my first time?"

The planchette moved in a small circle. Ashley held her breath watching it. Her fingers were barely touching the planchette and she peered at the other three hands for telltale signs they were pushing or pulling on it. But like her, they barely grazed it with their fingertips.

The planchette moved to the letter "M" and then to the "I." Ashley glanced at Maya. Her sister's mouth had fallen open watching the board. The planchette jerked to the "N" and then back to the "I." Mini? It shot back to the "G" and then the "O." It slid slower to the "L" and then even more slowly, back to the "F."

Ashley looked over at her sister. "Mini golf? Mom took you to mini golf? She took me to Chuck E. Cheese after my first visit."

Preston gazed at Maya. "Ih...it's true?"

Maya's eyes glistened with tears when she nodded. "Yeah. She offered ice cream but my mouth was sore. We were driving by Mini Putt Place and she just pulled in. She taught me how to play and laughed when I knocked the ball into the clown's mouth. I can still see her doing that."

Henry leaned forward looking at the board. "Still...it could have been you, Maya, pushing the planchette. You knew the answer."

This time it was Preston who came to her defense. "Stop it, He... Henry! She wu...wouldn't do that. And I would have fe...felt it if she ha...had."

Ashley could only stare at the board. She'd played on that mini golf course and could picture the clown that Maya was talking about. It was kind of like that horrible clown in the *It* movie she'd seen just this past year after Leah had pleaded with her to go. The fact that Maya even remembered the small detail of getting the ball in the clown's mouth resonated with truth.

Could the board really be working? Could their mother's spirit be there, answering the question?

Leah broke the silence that had descended like a shroud. "Is there anything more you want to ask your mother, Maya?"

Ashley knew there was. That was the whole point of this, to give Maya some peace after what had happened that fateful night.

Maya nodded and swiped a tear from her cheek. "I'm sorry, Mom. I miss you and Daddy." She sniffed. "Do you forgive me for the awful things I said to you...that night?"

This time, Henry shifted closer and his hand joined the others. He looked at Ashley, and the look in his eyes was a bit sheepish.

The planchette sat still, just vibrating a little which could have been just from their fingertips.

Leah looked at Henry. "Maybe you shouldn't do this. It worked before, after you left it."

Henry's chin rose, and he pulled his hand back. You could tell he was miffed but he held his tongue.

The planchette started to move, again very slowly.

A noise downstairs of the screen door banging made Ashley jump. Her aunt called out as she walked up the stairs. "How's that game going?"

Leah almost pulled the planchette from everyone's fingers getting it to move to the word "Goodbye."

Maya jumped up and flipped the light on and then scrambled to get back while Ashley shoved the board under the bed. It was a concerted effort with Henry shuffling the deck of cards and dealing them out.

Leah yelled looking over at the doorway, "I'm cleaning their clocks, Claire!"

Claire's footsteps sounded in the hallway and then she stood in the open doorway. "Henry's brother is downstairs." But instead of smiling and teasing them, her eyes were puzzled looking at each of them.

Uh oh. Aunt Claire wasn't stupid. She knew that they'd been up to something.

EIGHT

Henry took his cell phone from his pocket and looked at it. "Shit! Where'd that hour go?" He jumped to his feet and turned to Preston. "C'mon bud, we'd better get moving."

Ashley and Leah were next, making a beeline for the door, brushing by Claire. Ashley heard her aunt step into the room and speak, "Maya? Are you all right, honey?"

Shit! She probably knew Maya had been crying. Why would she cry if they'd just been playing a game of cards? Ashley paused at the top stair and listened.

Maya spoke next, "I'm fine. Except for my eye. I think I may have some dirt in it. Can you take a look and see?"

Ashley let out a whoosh of relief. Trust Maya to come up with something so fast. "Maya! Henry and Preston are leaving! Don't you want to say goodbye?"

"Coming!" Maya flew out the doorway, and her eyebrows bobbed high sharing a look with her sister.

That had been a close call. Ashley could hear the kids downstairs and especially Leah, her voice sweet as milk chocolate saying hi to Mason, asking him about his year away.

Ashley watched her aunt come out of Maya's room. She flashed a smile at Claire before adjusting the neckline of her shirt and walking downstairs behind Maya. Her aunt didn't seem concerned now. Claire had seemed to be stifling a chuckle. Whew!

Now for the next crisis. Mason Sherwood.

She smiled and took a deep breath. When she got to the bottom and went into the kitchen, that same breath froze in her chest. He was even better looking than she'd remembered, if that was possible. He turned, and under a tousled lock of dark hair on his forehead, his azure-blue eyes locked with hers. And he'd grown too! He had to be almost six feet tall and the sleeves of his T-shirt were stretched over lean, tanned muscle.

"Hi Mason." Ashley finally found her voice even if it had come out kind of squeaky.

"Ashley?" The corners of his mouth curled up and then he chuckled. "It's the braces. You don't have braces on your teeth anymore. That's what's different."

She shook her head. "Got them off last year." He'd noticed her back then? Well, he sure was noticing her right now. His gaze lingered, forgetting Henry and the others.

Leah interrupted the moment. "So you work at Gas Rite? That's pretty cool to get a summer job so quick. You just got back here." She stepped in closer to him, blocking the line of Ashley's sight.

He looked down at Leah. "It's okay, I guess." He turned to Henry. "You ready, little bro? You'd better go out and load your bikes."

Maya entered the room and looked up at Mason. "Too bad you had to work. We had a campfire and roasted weenies. You should drop by for a swim sometime." She turned and winked at Ashley before heading across the room and out the side door after the boys.

Mason looked over at Ashley. "So you guys just moved in, huh? It's a nice spot."

Leah once more interjected, "Maya's right about the swimming. We'd love it if you came by for a swim with us."

Ashley smiled but inside she ground her teeth together. Leah was acting like it was her house, asking Mason out there. Talk about pushy and obvious. "Yeah. The dock needs some work but the swimming is pretty good. Next time if you're out picking Henry up, bring your suit."

Claire had finished in the bathroom upstairs, and her feet sounded on the stairs behind Ashley. She nudged Ashley forward into the kitchen, following right on her heels. "So Mason, do you think you'll stay for the school year or go back to Wilmington?"

He huffed a sigh but smiled. "Haven't decided yet. My girlfriend is in Wilmington and she wants me to come back. I don't know. Saranac is closer to Whiteface." He looked at Ashley. "Do you ski?"

Leah jumped in with both feet. "I love skiing! I've only been a few times, but it's so much fun."

Had she even taken her eyes off the poor guy, gaping up at him like a lost puppy? Ashley stepped closer even though her heart had picked up a beat, and her palms were suddenly sweaty. "I used to ski with Mom and Dad all the time. But not so much the last couple of years."

Claire slipped by them and stood with her hand on the fridge door. "We're going to change that Ashley. I want to get back into skiing as well." She looked at Mason, "Would you like a soda or glass of water?"

He shook his head. "No thanks. I better get going and get Henry and Preston home. I've got work in the morning." He started across the room and then paused at the door, turning, "I might take you up on a swim sometime, Ashley. Maybe I should get your cell number. Just to make sure you're here and it's okay."

For once Leah held her tongue. Ashley smiled at her friend and then prattled off her cell number. He'd asked for her number! Okay, it was only for swimming, and he did have a girlfriend, but still. *Mason Sherwood asked for her number.*

***

It was almost an hour later before Leah thawed enough to talk to her and Maya. Leah had been quiet and had taken a long time to brush her teeth and get ready for bed.

Leah wore a long T-shirt, and her face was cleaned of any makeup when she came into Ashley's room. "He's not all that great looking...not really. He had a big zit on his forehead. It was like Cyclops looking back at me."

Ashley knew better than to argue. Sometimes Leah could sulk for hours, and it was a drag being around her. "He's already got a girlfriend anyway. Who cares about him. I doubt he's gonna stay around after the summer."

Maya appeared in the doorway in her sleeping shorts and T-shirt. Under her arm was the Ouija board. "Do you want to try this again? I mean we never really had that much time. Just when it started to work, Aunt Claire interrupted, and Mason and..." She looked like she'd cry if they turned her down.

Ashley sighed inwardly. Between Leah's sulking and Maya's ache for their parents, the evening was becoming a real downer. Still, she nodded. "Okay. But just for a little while, all right?"

Maya's eyes lit up, "I know that was Mom! How else could anyone know about the mini golf? It had to be her." For a moment her face was puzzled. "But why would she still be hanging around? I thought you died and then went to heaven if you led a good life. And for sure, she and Dad had."

Leah took the board from Maya and once more she set it on the floor for them. "Sometimes when people die prematurely like your parents, they are confused about their death. They've got unfinished business, issues that keep them tied to this realm. In your parents' case, you two may be keeping them from crossing over."

Ashley was torn. Part of her wanted to believe that it had been her mother earlier who'd connected with them through the board and another part was still skeptical, like Henry. "Is it possible that if there was a spirit they'd be able to read Maya's mind for the answer? Maybe it wasn't Mom. Maybe it was Maya subconsciously moving the gizmo."

Maya shook her head quickly. "It wasn't me, Ash. I swear it." She lowered and knelt next to Leah. "Can you get the lights? Light a candle this time too."

Ashley got up and went over to her dresser where a scented candle sat. She lit it and then flicked the overhead light off. With only the candle, it was even darker than when they'd done this is Maya's room. She hunkered down completing the circle; the three of them hunched around the board. The sound of her aunt and Carol downstairs in the kitchen was a dull backdrop to the quiet in the room. They'd killed one bottle of wine and had started on another. From the odd peal of laughter, they probably were content to stay there for another hour or so. There was little chance that they'd come up to check on them.

Shadow licked the underside of Leah's cheeks while her eyes sparked looking at Ashley and Maya. She placed her fingertips on the planchette that she'd placed under the arc of letters. "Do you want me to ask the questions, or will you do it Maya?"

Maya shook her head. "You start. When Mom comes, I'll take over." She placed her fingers on the object next to Ashley's.

Leah took a deep breath. "We are seeking the spirit of Gail Vincent. If you are here, please give us a sign that it is you. Please tell us. Your daughters wish to communicate with you, Gail."

Ashley watched the planchette, waiting, hoping it would move. She could hear Maya breathing, see her fingers waver a little, lightly brushing the small reader. Again, it seemed to take many minutes for anything to happen. She jerked a little when the object slid to the word "Yes."

Maya's voice was a whisper, "Mom? You know I'm sorry for what I said, don't you? Please let me know that you forgive me."

The planchette moved away from the "Yes" and then slid back, hovering above it. And the light in the room grew brighter. Ashley looked up at the candle where the flame had flared higher. The fire shot to the side burning in a horizontal flash as if moved by a breeze, but the air was deathly still.

Her heart sped up and she turned to peer into Leah's eyes. "Is that..."

Leah nodded. "She's here, Maya. She's giving you another sign that she forgives you."

Maya's lower lip quivered. "Mom. I miss you and Daddy so much." She took a breath, and her voice was stronger when she spoke, "Are you okay?"

Ashley fought her own tears. She had never expected this to work but when the candle flickered and changed on its own she knew that something was there. And it had to be her mother. "Mom? Is Daddy with you? It's Ashley, Mom."

"She knows that, Ash. Is there anything else you want to add to Maya's question?" Leah's face was solemn when she gazed at her.

Ashley shook her head. "I guess we can only ask one question at a time with this thing. Maya's question is a good one."

Maya repeated it, "Are you okay, Mom? Where are you?"

The planchette moved to the "W" and then to the "I." Slowly it crept through the letters "T," "H," "Y," "O" and "U" before stopping.

Maya's eyes glistened with tears looking over at her sister. "She's with us, Ashley!"

Ashley leaned closer to the board. "Is Daddy there?"

The planchette began to move toward the "Yes" but then spun down the board to the "Goodbye" so fast it left Ashley's fingers.

She looked over at Leah. "What happened?"

Leah's eyes practically popped out onto her cheekbones they were so big. She shook her head slowly, "I don't know. Why would she break contact so quickly?"

NINE

Downstairs, Claire noticed the lights flicker a couple times. She looked at the refrigerator wondering if it had kicked in causing that.

Carol set her glass of wine down. "It looks like you may have to do something with the wiring, Claire. That was kind of odd."

Claire nodded. "Yeah maybe the panel needs to be updated while I'm changing things. God knows when we use the dryer and get a dishwasher, we'll probably need a bigger electrical service." She picked up the wine, about to top Carol's glass but Carol waved her away.

"I've had enough, thanks." Carol looked down at the table for a moment. "So, has Lucas seen the house? What's he think?"

Claire sat back and felt the muscles in the back of her neck tighten. Carol didn't like Lucas much, so there had to be a reason for her to bring him into their conversation. "Nope. He's coming out tomorrow for dinner. I wanted to do the move with the girls on my own."

"Is he still bugging you about moving in together?" Carol

frowned.

"Kind of. He wasn't thrilled that I bought this place. But he needs to understand I want my space. After five years of marriage to Jake, I've enjoyed my independence for the last two years."

Carol snorted. "Not really independence when you've got your nieces in tow." She leaned forward. "I mean, you took them in right around the time you guys split up."

"I wouldn't have it any other way." Claire picked at the label of the wine bottle, gazing absently at her fingernail. "The funny and not funny ha ha thing, is that having kids was the reason Jake and I broke up." She snorted. "He wanted them and I didn't. I think he thought I'd change after we were married." She shrugged. "Well, I did but much too late for us."

"Have you heard from him since the divorce? Is he still in Syracuse?"

Claire shook her head. "I thought of calling him when Robert and Gail died. But I didn't. The girls needed me so much, and it was hard on me too. Rob was my only living relative. Well, around here at least. We have a cousin in Florida. But I haven't seen him since I was six."

She sighed picturing Rob. "My big brother used to watch over me. And now I'm watching over his kids."

"And Lucas? How does he feel about the girls? Somehow I can't picture him as a family guy." Carol's face had set into a sneer which she probably wasn't even aware of. There was nothing phony about Carol which was part of her charm to Claire's way of thinking.

"Oh, he's okay with kids as long as they're his. He's Italian with that whole lineage thing." Claire got up and poured a glass of water. "He's hinted that maybe the girls would be better off with my cousin. He thinks I should look him up to see if he has a family."

"Blood is thicker than water, Claire. You love these girls like they were your own. You can't go foisting them off for some guy you've known only a little over a year." The muscle in Carol's cheek twitched.

Claire flopped down into the chair and looked over at her friend. Even though they'd only been friends for a short time, Carol was her closest confident and ally. "Don't worry I wouldn't in a million years consider it. You know, even without the girls I'd still say no to Lucas with his plans to shack up or get married. I really do need my own space for a bit longer."

Carol smiled. "You sure you're really over Jake? I've never met the guy, but your voice is always sad when you talk about him."

"Sometimes I wonder that as well. But he's moved on. And so should I."

Carol looked away for a moment and chewed her lower lip. She turned back and said, "I saw Lucas in the casino this week. He didn't see me, but he was with a young blond. She couldn't have been more than nineteen."

Claire's face froze. "*Nineteen*?"

Carol made a small shrug. "Maybe older, but only a little bit. She was dressed like a skank and looked trashy." She sighed.

"But he doesn't like the casino! He told me!" The only time she'd suggested going there for a change of pace, he'd shut her down fast. He'd said it was boring and loud, not to mention probably rigged as well. Why would he be there and apparently not on his own? "You're sure you saw Lucas there?"

"Yeah, I'm sure. He didn't see me as I was coming out of the office, and he was at the blackjack table with that hooker. But it was him all right."

"A hooker!" Oh my God. It was even worse. He was with a hooker? Claire's mouth fell open. "Maybe he wasn't with her. She could have just been hustling him. That had to be it." Still she was going to ask him about it.

"Look, I grew up in Chicago. I know hookers and how they operate. I'm pretty sure he was with her." Carol sat back and folded her arms over her chest. "I'm just saying I think you can do better than Lucas Moretti. I know he's handsome, and he has a nice place, but there's something about him. Hedge fund manager! Hah! If he was really in the stock market why isn't he in the Big Apple? Saranac Lake isn't exactly Wall Street."

Claire squared her shoulders. "You don't have to be on Wall Street to do investment work, Carol. With the internet you can live anywhere and be connected. Frankly, I'm surprised you don't work from home. I mean the casino is an hour away, and in winter the commute can't be much fun."

"I do work from home sometimes. But I like going in to work. Aside from the free meals it's nice to see my friends in the office." Carol stood up and stretched. "I'm going to get my stuff from the jeep. And then crash on your sofa. I kind of feel bad I didn't do all that much to help you today." She took a deep breath. "I'll make up for it tomorrow, I promise."

Claire's head tipped to the side gazing up at her friend. "Just having you out here and us enjoying a night to ourselves is enough. We should make this a weekly thing."

"You say that all the time and then you end up canceling at the last minute."

Claire rose and put her hand on Carol's shoulder. "Only when I'm working. People want to buy houses on their schedule, not mine, and being the sales agent…well, a girl's gotta eat. Especially with two teenagers to feed as well."

"Yeah, yeah," Carol called over her shoulder as she walked across the room to the side door.

When she left, Claire picked up the glasses and rinsed them in the sink. The thing with Lucas in the casino niggled in her gut. She was definitely going to find out more about that. A hooker? Lucas? No way.

Right?

TEN

The next morning a tap on the bedroom door yanked Ashley from a sound sleep. The door opened and Aunt Claire smiled at her. "I let you girls sleep as long as I could. I'm afraid there's just toast for breakfast till I get back from the supermarket." She stepped into the room and looked around, sniffing the air. "You girls burned a candle? I can smell the vanilla scent."

Leah rolled over and then sat up from her spot at the other side of the bed. "Hey Claire. What time is it?"

Claire glanced at her watch. "A little after nine. Carol is up and already starting the painting in the living room. Can you believe that?"

Ashley threw the covers back. "Wow! She's ambitious." She looked around the room for anything they may have missed from the night before. But she was sure Maya had taken the board to her room for safekeeping. None of them had wanted to continue with the session after the planchette had swooped to the "Goodbye." Thinking of it still made her uneasy.

"Well, if you want to pitch in to help Carol, I'm sure she wouldn't mind." Claire started to leave but then paused, "I'm picking up steak for dinner. Lucas is coming out to see the place and have dinner."

Ashley forced a smile she certainly didn't feel. Lucas was such a phony. Why couldn't Aunt Claire see it? She turned to Leah. "Are you sticking around for dinner? Spending another night here?" She crossed her fingers that Leah would.

Leah shook her head. "Sorry. I've got to babysit tonight for the Harding's. Mom is picking me up at five."

Aunt Claire turned when Maya joined her standing in the doorway. "Hey sunshine!" She gave Maya a kiss on the forehead before looking over at Leah. "Carol is going home this afternoon too. Maybe you could catch a ride with her and save your mom a trip."

"Thanks. I'll let her know." Leah got up and grabbed her phone.

"Well, I'm off! The sooner I leave, the sooner I'll be back to get some more stuff done." Claire slipped away, and her footsteps sounded on the stairs.

Maya looked up at Ashley. "Did I hear right, that Lucas is coming for dinner?" She slumped into the room and sat on the bed.

"Yeah." Ashley turned to Leah. "Need help babysitting?"

Before she could answer Maya pulled a pillow from the bed and hurled it at her sister. "No way. You're not deserting me here with *Puke Ass*."

"Shhh... I don't think she's left yet. You shouldn't call him that. It might slip out when he's here." Ashley tossed the pillow back at her sister. "It's just dinner. We can come upstairs right after."

Maya's eyes lit up as she hugged the pillow to her tummy, "Maybe we can do the Ouija board again. Aunt Claire will be busy with Puke Ass."

Leah was just ending the call and she looked at each of them. "I wouldn't do that without me here. I have more experience with this kind of stuff. The way the session ended last night was weird. I'm going to post it on Facebook to see if anyone else had something like that happen to them. It might mean something."

Ashley looked at Maya. There was no way Leah's warning was going to deter her sister from trying to contact their parents. It was obvious from the way she turned away, setting the pillow down and not even bothering to argue.

"Leah might be right, Maya. I think we should leave it alone. You contacted Mom I think and that's enough. Let it be. Maybe we should throw it away."

Maya's glared at her sister. "No! We didn't connect with Daddy. We should at least try to do that. Don't you want to know he's with Mom? Don't you want to talk to him?"

Leah touched Ashley's arm. "I can come out tomorrow if you want. Leave it till then. At least I'll know why it shut down so quickly last night. It's only one night to wait."

Ashley looked at Maya, waiting for her to agree, but Maya got up and just walked out of the room. She turned to Leah. "I'll talk to her." She rolled her eyes and then grabbed her robe from the back of the door. "I can't believe I'm actually going along with you on this but that question Maya asked...That was weird that the answer came up."

Leah followed her out of the room. "It works Ashley…but Maya shouldn't treat this lightly. From what I know, it's not always good spirits who come through. That's why you need me here. I can sense if it's going bad and can shut it down."

Ashley wasn't sure whether what Leah said was true. It could be just Leah trying to be self-important, being all melodramatic and all. It wouldn't be the first time she'd done something like that.

Leah was the typical middle child, with an older sister who had everything going for her—looks, wicked smart, and probably the most popular girl in their school—and then there was Preston. He'd always be the doted-on *baby* of the family. His speech impediment just brought more focus away from Leah's mother. Leah had missed out on her sister's looks and had to compete with a younger brother who was kinda challenged. So yeah, her making a big deal about the Ouija board was her chance for a spotlight…something that made her special.

Even so, Ashley had had enough of this subject. "I'll do what I can about the stupid Ouija board."

"It's *not* stupid, Ashley!"

"Okay, whatever. Hey, how about after we help Carol with the painting, why don't we explore the area around here? We'll hike down the road and see who lives at the end of it. There's got to be some hiking trails with all these woods around here."

Leah smiled. "Yeah. We'll see what's around and then go for a swim. Maybe we can bicycle. I could use Claire's bike."

***

A few hours later outside on the driveway, Maya wiped a line of sweat from her forehead before starting off on her bike. She shot a dirty look at Ashley beside her. "I still think we should have gone swimming before we did this."

"No one's forcing you to come you know!" Ashley pedaled harder to catch up with Leah. Maya could be so whiny sometimes. At least Maya didn't have asthma to contend with. Yet, you didn't see *her* complaining even if she did have to take her inhaler everywhere. And after being around paint fumes she'd had to use it a few times.

"You think I'm staying back there with Aunt Claire and Carol? They'd have me painting the laundry room! Enough painting for one day for this girl." Maya soon caught up and purposely wheeled her bike close to Ashley's, making it look like she was going to bang into her before veering off.

Leah stopped at the end of the driveway and looked up the road. "Hey Maya! Your boyfriends are coming out to see you again!"

Ashley stopped and in the distance she could see the two guys pedaling hard. Maya stopped next to her and smiled. "Maybe they'll go swimming with me instead of this."

"Mayan! Wait for us!" Henry's hair flew up off his forehead as his feet pumped the pedals fast.

Behind him, Preston's hand rose to wave.

When the pair came to a halt next to them, Henry spoke,

"Where are you going?"

Leah answered, "Exploring. We're just going down the road to see what's there. See if there's any hiking trails or anything interesting."

Maya groaned. "And they want to do that in this heat! You guys want to go swimming instead?" She smiled at Henry.

Preston moved his bike closer to her. "I...I'd like to see what's th...there. We can swi....swim after."

Henry nodded and pushed off on his bike leading the way. "Yeah. I've never been past this point. Let's see if anyone lives down there."

Ashley looked over at Leah and her voice was low, "That settles it for Maya, doesn't it? If Henry's going then..." Her foot pushed against the pedal.

The land bordering the road was mostly covered with thick stands of pine and spruce trees with an occasional birch or maple breaking the dark green. After a straight stretch that took a few minutes to ride, there was a bend in the road. When Ashley rounded it, she saw a small dilapidated cottage with an old, gray car parked in the driveway. Instead of a lawn, the yard was all dug up, made into a big garden, and an old woman was bent weeding in the rows of dirt. She rose to watch them pass, shielding her eyes from the sun. A tuft of white hair stuck out from the edge of a red kerchief that covered the rest of her head.

Leah pulled up alongside her and hissed a whisper, "That's the old gypsy woman! I didn't know she lived out here!"

Ashley turned her head to peer at the old woman. Of course she'd seen the woman in the small town. She was one of the town's *characters*. It was hard not to notice her when she shopped, always muttering in some foreign language and always wearing long skirts and mismatched sweaters no matter how hot it was. And there was that smell, a musty mothball scent trailing the old crone.

She turned back to Leah. "Oh my God. *That's* our nearest neighbor! Makes me kind of glad I don't have pets!"

Leah snickered. "You don't believe all that do you? That

she's some kind of witch sacrificing small animals? She's probably just demented." She grinned. "All the same, I'm glad she's *your* neighbor, not mine."

Ashley looked back at the old woman. It looked like the old lady lifted her hand to wave but it was hard to tell with the angle of the sun shining down on her. Ashley's shoulders fell watching the old woman. Maybe she was just eccentric, and she sure as hell didn't have much money, not from the looks of her house. It looked like a good gust of wind would knock it over.

When she was well past, she noticed Henry and Preston stopped, laying their bikes down on the side of the road. Maya threw hers down and joined them, racing into the stand of trees. Ashley looked over at Leah. "Wonder what they found."

She pedaled fifty feet or so and then stopped, peering at the break in the trees and a worn path.

Leah set the bike down and then walked over to it. "C'mon. Let's check it out."

Ashley raced over to join her, before she disappeared into the stand of trees. "Maya! Wait!" She peered at the wire fence lining the property, broken with strands of rusty metal reaching out like fingers at each side of the path. But there was no sign posted that it was private property. She followed Leah, being careful not to let the wire scrape her bare arms.

The scent of the trees and loam underneath was warm and moist in her nostrils. The air was close and thick, making it hard to breath. She grabbed her inhaler and took a deep puff, filling her lungs.

"Holy shit! Look at this!" Henry's voice drifted back to them.

When she and Leah rounded a bend there was a clearing. A perfect circle of soft grass was dappled from the sunbeams threading through the branches of the trees ringing it. Maya and the guys were sprawled on the grass, their arms and legs spread like they were making snow angels, except this was plush green instead of a fresh mound of snow.

Leah turned to her and her eyes were filled with horror. She looked over at her brother and Maya. "Get out of there! That's a fairy circle! You're not supposed to go in it!"

"What?" Ashley looked around at the perfect circle about twenty feet across. There was no logical reason for it to be there, not when the growth of trees and brush was so dense surrounding it. It was weird but a *fairy circle*?

Maya sat up and looked over at Leah. "What are you talking about? This is neat! It's just perfect. A perfect clearing surrounded—"

"It isn't! Don't you feel it? The air isn't right. It's too still and thick. This is a *fairy circle*. Why else would there be nothing but grass here? Get out of there, guys! Now!" Leah yelled, and her hands were balled fists. "Preston!"

Maya sat up and looked over at Preston. "Your sister is seriously crazy sometimes." She'd muttered it but still in the quiet air it had echoed over for Ashley to hear.

Preston nodded while Henry jumped up. His strides were wide, almost leaping and dancing at the edge of the clearing, "Look at me! I'm Peter Pan!" He darted in and grabbed Maya's hand. "C'mon Tinkerbell! Let's make like the fairies!"

"Stop it, Henry!" Leah shouted, and then turned to Ashley for support.

"Le...let's go guys. I...I don't feel guh...good." Preston got up and walked over to his sister.

"Maya! C'mon. Enough fooling around." For some reason Ashley didn't feel good about being there anymore. And watching Henry's antics, his jeers seemed wrong.

Leah turned slightly, about to leave but before she did she yelled once more, "Fine! But this is super bad luck to do what you're doing, Henry! And you too, Maya!" She spun on her heels, and Ashley could hear her feet thudding on the path.

Maya pulled away from Henry. "Cut it out." She looked over at Ashley as she walked out of the clearing. "I told you we should have gone swimming." She brushed by her sister, sprinting to catch up to Preston and Leah.

Henry muttered as he joined her at the edge, "Geez, I was just kidding around. Everyone's acting like I farted in church or something."

Ashley looked around at the clearing. It had sure put a damper on the afternoon with Leah getting all huffy. Still, it wasn't a place that she'd want to visit anytime soon. It was definitely odd to say the least.

She took another hit of the inhaler as she walked along the path trying to catch up to the others. They were well ahead of her on their bikes racing despite the heat of the day. She took her time pedaling down the old road. When the old lady's house came into view she noticed the woman walking down her laneway shouting at the others who were abreast, gliding by. It only made them bike faster to get away.

Great. It was about fifty feet away and she'd have to face the old lady, alone. What was with her, yelling like that? She steered to the far side of the road, so that she wouldn't be near her. Trying to ignore her as she got closer, Ashley stared straight ahead. But the woman stepped onto the road raising her arm to flag Ashley down while yelling some gibberish.

Ashley's eyes grew wider, and she almost fell from the bike before pumping her legs hard to get away. The woman yelled one last time at Ashley's back but it was far enough behind her that she breathed a sigh of relief. What the hell was wrong with the old bat? She didn't own the road and they were just riding by, not bothering her.

When she got around the bend, the others were waiting. Maya's mouth fell open and she let out a nervous laugh. "We thought she had you! What the hell is up with her?"

Leah glared at her. "You think *I'm* crazy? That woman is totally bat shit. I wonder if this has anything to do with that fairy circle?"

Ashley snorted. "It wouldn't surprise me. Remind me not to go to *her* house this Halloween."

"Le...let's keep guh...going. In ca...case she comes after us." Preston hopped on his bike and started up the road. "Cuh...c'mon, Maya!"

Henry and Maya weren't far behind him while Leah held back keeping Ashley company. She looked over at Ashley.

"I've never seen the old bat upset like that. She was really bent out of shape seeing us ride by. I wish I knew what she was yelling."

Ashley rolled her eyes. "I'm sure it wasn't anything nice from the look on her face. She actually tried to stop me, coming out on the road. I almost fell off my bike!"

The end of the driveway was just up ahead, with Maya and the boys turning into it. Ashley turned to Leah. "I'll mention this to Aunt Claire. She wouldn't want to run into that old witch if she's ever out jogging down this road."

"Yeah, good thinking. Let's get changed into our bathing suits. I'm melting in this heat." Leah pushed ahead and propped the bike against the side of the house.

Fifteen minutes later they were changed with towels draped over their necks coming out the back door. Carol and Aunt Claire were taking a break lounging in lawn chairs near the shore. Maya and the guys were already swimming, not even bothering to change into bathing suits. They were a little past the dock and the air rang with their taunts to each other.

Ashley paused next to her aunt. "You know that crazy, old lady we've seen shopping downtown? The one who always mutters and wears a scarf on her head like some kind of gypsy?"

"I know who you mean. Mrs. Kovac, that's her name. What about her?" Aunt Claire swatted a fly away and then peered up at her.

"She lives just down the road, around the bend."

Leah's finger made a circle in the air next to her temple. "She is really round the bend, if you know what I mean."

Ashley continued, "She started yelling at us and even came out in the road after me. She's got some serious anger issues."

Aunt Claire's head tipped to the side. "I knew she lived out this way, but I didn't know she was that close. She's Romanian. Her husband died years ago. She probably has a right to be a little unhinged from what I know. Some bad things happened to them during the war."

This time it was Carol who spoke, "The Jews weren't the

only ones persecuted by the Nazis. Gypsies were rounded up too. I think she's pretty harmless from what I've seen. But maybe you should avoid going near her place. You probably upset her as much as she did to you."

Ashley shook her head and snorted. "You don't have to tell me twice." She was about to turn when a sharp yelp rang through the air.

Henry's face contorted as he swam toward the shore. Maya and Preston looked confused but they followed him. When he got to the spot where he could stand, he pulled his leg up out of the water. A ribbon of blood coated the sole of his foot.

"What happened?" Aunt Claire rose to her feet while Ashley and Leah rushed out to him.

Henry grimaced. "I stepped on a sharp rock or something. I was underwater and pushed myself up and something cut into my foot."

Ashley and Leah each took an arm, draping it over their shoulder and helping him hobble to the shore. He flopped down on the grass to examine his injury. "Hmm...it's funny, but my foot—it's not that hot sting kind of feeling like when I've gotten cuts before this. My foot feels cold." He rubbed the top. "*Really* cold."

Leah looked over at Ashley. There was no need for words in the silent communication.

It was Henry who had poked fun in the fairy circle. It was Henry who had been hurt.

ELEVEN

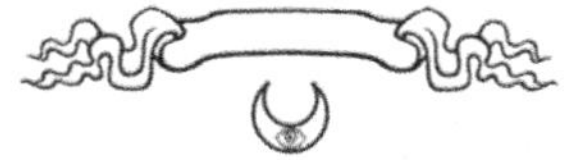

It was around five that Ashley stood in the driveway alongside Claire waving goodbye as Carol's jeep backed out.

Claire turned to her. "I've got to get changed into something decent. Lucas will be out soon." She turned and looked where Henry and Preston were huddled with Maya on the lawn. "I hope Henry's foot doesn't get infected. Maybe I should have insisted on taking him home."

Ashley shook her head. "You tried, Aunt Claire. He's stubborn. Plus he didn't want to seem weak in front of Maya. Mason will give him and Preston a lift home. I'm sure if he thinks Henry needs a stitch in that foot he'll take him to emergency or a clinic."

Her aunt sighed. "I feel so bad. Like it's my fault. From now on, you guys are wearing water shoes when you go swimming." She was about to leave but her lips twitched in a smile, "Good thing Mason's job is nearby to pick his brother up...again."

"He's got a girlfriend, Aunt Claire." Ashley felt her face grow warm, and she looked down, kicking at a stone in the driveway.

"She's in Wilmington. And he sure wasn't thinking of her when he asked for your cell number last night." This time Aunt Claire outright grinned. "But even if he's taken, he seems like a nice guy to have as a friend."

"Yeah, I guess." Ashley was still a little disappointed but she managed a smile. "I'd better get Maya. We should get out of these wet bathing suits."

She wandered over and looked down at Maya and the boys. "How's the foot, Henry?"

"It's fine. It's just a cut. Although it's gonna make riding my bike kind of hard for a day or so." He looked up at her, his dark eyes grinning. She could see the resemblance to Mason in the smile and set of his chin. It was no wonder Maya liked him.

"If you come out for a swim again, you have to wear water shoes. Aunt Claire's new rule."

Preston nodded. "For shu...sure. Funny to hit that ruh...rock when the buh...bottom's kind of silty."

Maya shot a look at him. "You're still thinking of that fairy circle, Pres? It's just coincidence that Henry got hurt. Not everything is supernatural like Leah would have us think."

At the sound of a car driving up the driveway, Ashley turned. She groaned inwardly seeing the red sports car. Lucas was here and he was early.

"Puke Ass." It was barely audible. Maya's whispered name for him.

"Can you go let Aunt Claire know he's here? Get changed out of that wet suit when you're in there, Maya. I'll go say hi." She started out, her feet feeling heavier with each step toward him.

Lucas got out and waved before looking up at the house and over to the lake. "Hi Ashley. You girls enjoying the place?" His arms crossed over his chest and his legs spread standing there waiting. His sunglasses crowned the top of his head and his eyes darted around at the property.

"Hi Lucas. Yeah, it's okay." She paused as he came across the lawn to meet her. Even the way he walked was annoying—

kind of cocky like he owned the place.

He stopped next to the boys and looked down at them, "I didn't know you guys lived nearby. Say, what's with the foot?" He looked at the bandage wrapped around Henry's foot.

"I got attacked by piranha fish!"

"What?"

Henry laughed. "Gotcha'! It's just a cut, that's all. I stepped on a sharp rock when we were swimming." Henry rose to his feet, testing his hurt foot on the soft grass. "My brother's coming to pick us up." He looked at Lucas. "You're in investments aren't you? You must be making a killing on the market right now with the recent surge."

Ashley did a double groan inside. Henry was fascinated by anything to do with banking and investment. Most kids his age read Harry Potter. Henry read the *Wall Street Journal.* She shot a look at Preston only to see the same slump in his shoulders knowing that Henry was about to go into some sort of investment spiel.

Lucas nodded. "Yeah, things are good in the market all right."

He started to turn away, looking at Ashley, but Henry continued, "What company do you use on the floor?"

"I do everything myself."

Henry's face brightened. "You got your own seat? Where?"

"Wherever I plant my butt, man." Lucas looked away before turning to Ashley. "What's your aunt doing?"

Before she had a chance to reply, Henry peppered Lucas with another question, "What's your position with treasuries? Are you shorting? We're about two ticks from serious trouble right?" Henry peered at him, his face a picture of earnest interest.

Lucas's eyes widened and he sputtered, "Don't let all that doomsday clock nonsense scare ya kid. Two ticks, ten ticks, there ain't going to be any wars; nothing's gonna blow up." When Henry stared at him, Lucas cut the conversation short. He turned to Ashley. "I think I'll go in and make myself a drink and see what Claire's doing." With that he hustled across the lawn to the back door.

Henry's face was in a knot watching Lucas depart. "That guy's a hedge fund manager? Remind me never to give him any money to invest."

"Yu...you don't ha...have any money, Henry." Preston laughed as he got to his feet.

Henry spun on him. "He didn't know what the hell I was talking about, bud! The ticks I was referring to wasn't the doomsday clock. It was fractional percentage points on bonds. He should have known that." He looked at the door Lucas had gone through. "Shit. He probably thinks a T-bill is some kind of steak!"

Preston's cheeks seemed to color a bit, and he quickly countered, "You don't th...think he's le...legit?"

Henry's face clouded. "No… I don't think he is. When I asked him who he uses on the floor, he said he did it all himself!"

"So?"

Henry rolled his eyes. "You can't! Each exchange—NYSE, NASDAQ, all of them have listed brokers who have seats on the exchange and you gotta trade through them!" He looked back at the house where Lucas went in. "That guy says he's a fund manager and doesn't even know the basic terms?" He shook his head. "No. Way." He looked back to Preston. "He doesn't do business with Wall Street, that's for sure."

"Bu..but…"

Henry looked at Ashley and then he shrugged. "I don't know where he makes his money. Look at his car. He has money obviously, but it's not from investments."

Ashley looked over at the door which banged shut after Lucas. He had sure hightailed it away when Henry started asking questions. What was Puke Ass up to?

But she didn't have long to think about it when the sound of another vehicle's tires rolling over the gravel caught her attention. She turned and saw a black pickup truck come to a stop, towering over the small sports car. Mason got out and waved to them before walking over.

He smiled at Ashley. "Hey there! Didn't think I'd be back so soon!" His smile fell when he looked at Henry. "Cut your foot, huh? It must be pretty bad that you couldn't ride your bike. Let me have a look at it."

Henry sank back onto the grass and started peeling the bandage away, "I don't think it's that bad. I just thought I'd make it worse and the bleeding would start again if I applied any pressure with my foot on the bike pedal."

Mason went down to one knee and took Henry's foot in his hand, peering at the slash. It was about an inch long and had sliced through a few layers of skin. Just the pressure of Mason's fingers near it made a line of blood gush from the wound.

"Aunt Claire wanted to take him in to have it looked at but—"

"I don't think they could put a stitch there. Not on the sole of his foot." Mason rewrapped the bandage around Henry's foot. "You'll live. But we'll put some antiseptic on it when we get home and change the bandage." He reached out and pulled Henry up from the grass.

"More antiseptic? Claire already doused my foot with it."

The screen door banged and then Maya sprinted over. "Hi Mason. You guys are leaving now?" She'd changed into a jean skirt and tank top and pulled her damp hair back into a ponytail. It made Ashley feel pretty self-conscious standing around in her tankini.

Preston spoke, "Yeah. Re...remember your aunt said wuh...we could bu...build a raft?"

Maya nodded. "Yeah. What about it?"

Preston turned to Mason. "Thu...there's some plastic ba...barrels that my neighbor sa...said I could have. We only nee...need four. And we've got a sheet of ply...plywood in our garage. You cu...could bring them out, maybe?" He looked over at Maya. "If your aunt can buy four, two by ten pine buh...boards and a couple tuh...two by fours, we could buh...build it. I luh...looked it up on the ih...internet."

Ashley grinned. Preston had this all figured out. He'd do

anything to spend more time out there with Maya.

Mason smiled. "Sure I'll bring them out for you. If you can wait till Tuesday when I'm off, I'll help you build it. And..." He looked at Ashley. "...We've got some lumber left over from the deck we built last year. We can use that and save your aunt buying more."

"Cool!" Maya's face lit up. She glanced over at her sister before looking back at Mason. "You can stay for dinner afterward. It's the least we can do since we're getting a free raft."

Ashley thought if her chest expanded anymore she was going to float off into space. Especially when Mason looked at her and nodded. His whole face seemed to light up when he spoke, "Make that burgers, and it's a date. I mean deal."

Had that been a slip of the tongue or had he just kind of, sort of, asked her on a date? Okay, there would be a bunch of people there too, but still....

She smiled. "Like Maya said, it'll be fun. But remember your water shoes." She kicked herself mentally. 'Remember your water shoes?' Brilliant comeback.

"Hello?" Henry shot a look at everyone in turn. "If you're finished making plans to build the ark, I need to get going. Remember?" He pointed a finger down. "Amputated foot?"

Mason looped Henry's arm over his shoulder and smiled down at him. "Like you'd ever let us forget." He looked over at Ashley. "I'd better get going. See you Tuesday."

"Can't wait!" It popped out of her mouth before her brain had a chance to engage. Immediately her cheeks warmed, but Mason's smile only grew bigger.

"Suh...see you later, Maya!" Preston went to Henry's other side helping him limp across the lawn.

Maya turned to Ashley and in a low voice, "Wasn't that clever of me? Asking Mason to dinner?" Her grin was impish as she nudged her sister with her shoulder.

"And Henry being here too would have nothing to do with it, right?" Ashley looked over at the back door where Lucas and her aunt were coming out. The wind whooshed out of her sails. "I wish it were Tuesday and this dinner with Puke Ass was over."

"Me too."

***

The dinner was...*odd.*

Something was up with Aunt Claire. Normally she laughed a lot even if Lucas's attempt at humor wasn't all that funny. She was still nice, but when she talked to Lucas there was a reserve in her manner. Aunt Claire was fine with Maya and her but there was a definite strain when she talked to Lucas. She glanced at Maya, but her sister's face didn't register as anything except mild boredom.

Aunt Claire finished her glass of wine and smiled at Lucas. Well, her mouth smiled but not her eyes. "So what did you do for excitement this week? Don't tell me you worked nonstop. That's not good for anyone. All work and no play and all that."

He jerked back slightly but then his smile returned, "You know me. I'm a self confessed workaholic." His hand covered hers. "Besides, if you're not with me I'd just as soon work. It's not only profitable, but the time passes more quickly."

Aunt Claire looked down at his hand and then pulled hers away, shifting back in her chair. "Oh? You stayed put all week? No night out at all?"

His eyes narrowed and he leaned in. "Well, I may have went to the store for a few things. Filled up the car with gas...that's about it. Why do you ask?"

Aunt Claire looked over at Ashley and Maya. "If you girls are done, you may be excused."

Ashley's eyes widened but she rose to her feet. Her aunt wasn't even asking them to clear the table? It was obvious that whatever she had to say to Lucas, she didn't want them there. Shit. It looked like he was in trouble and she couldn't get to watch.

"C'mon, Ash." Maya smiled and almost skipped out of the

room.

"You don't want me to stack the dishes?" Ashley lingered a little, her gaze flitting between Lucas and her aunt.

"No. Not tonight. I'll get them." Her aunt's face was set, not even a smile.

Ashley shrugged and then walked across the kitchen to join her sister. She squeezed Maya's arm and pulled her toward the stairs, "I think there's trouble in paradise. Didn't you catch the chilly vibes from Aunt Claire?"

Maya's eyes twinkled. "We can only hope." She darted up the stairs ahead of Ashley. "Let's get the you-know-what out."

Oh God. Not the Ouija board. And after Leah warned them too.

TWELVE

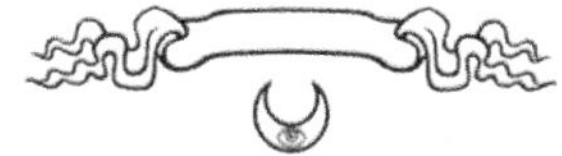

Ashley hurried after her sister. "Maya!" When she got to her sister's bedroom the younger girl was bent over grabbing the board from the dresser drawer. Ashley went into the room and closed the door behind her. "Remember what Leah said. We should wait till she's here tomorrow."

As if Leah was somehow telepathically connected, Ashley's cell phone vibrated with a text message.

"How's the dinner going?"

She grit her teeth and her fingers flew typing an answer.

"I wish I knew. I think Aunt Claire is mad at him. We just came upstairs."

Maya pulled her curtain closed to dim the room from the fading sunset outside. She stepped over to the bed and opened the box, setting the board before her. "C'mon Ash."

The cell phone buzzed again with another message.

"I hope you're not using that board. What

happened last night was bad. I told my Facebook group about it."

Ashley looked over at Maya. "She says that what happened last night was bad."

Maya's face screwed up into a scowl. "What's that supposed to mean? Bad. Let's just do this. She doesn't have to know. Tell her you're going to take a shower or something and can't talk." Maya set the planchette on the board and placed her fingertips on it.

Ashley sighed. Maya was going to do this with or without her it seemed. She turned the cell phone on "Airplane mode" and then went over to join her sister. She wasn't going to lie to Leah, not if she could help it. But on the other hand, Leah was acting so high and mighty it was downright annoying.

She looked over at Maya. "I'll do this with you, but I'm asking the questions. If something like last night happens, we quit this for good, okay?"

Maya nodded.

Ashley's fingers rested on the small wooden reader and she took a deep breath. "If you're out there Mom or Dad, can you let us know." She waited, staring at the reader.

"You're supposed to ask for benign spirits, Ash. That's what Leah did."

She huffed an irritated sigh. "Fine. If there are benign spirits here, please communicate with us. Is anyone here?"

The planchette began to vibrate a little and then slid in a small circle in the center of the board. Ashley looked over at Maya and then back at the reader. "Is that you, Mom?"

The reader jerked to the "Yes" and stopped. It had happened so fast that Ashley's heart skipped a beat. She took a few breaths and continued, "Is Daddy with you?"

The planchette slid away from the "Yes" and then jerked back to it, coming to a stop. Her gaze fell to the side. What should she ask him? How could she be sure it was him? "Daddy, if that's you, tell me the name of my first softball coach." It was something that Maya wouldn't know since she'd been too young.

The planchette slid over to the letter "N," "I," "C" and then shot back to the "K." Nick! Yes! It had to be her father they were communicating with.

She felt tears sting the back of her eyes remembering the Saturday morning practices that her dad took her to, standing on the sidelines and shouting encouragement. She looked over at Maya and then swiped a tear from her eye.

"Ask him if he's happy?"

She shot a look at Maya. "How could he be happy? He's dead and we're here." She looked down at the planchette. "Are you at peace, Dad? With Mom?"

The planchette started doing circles again, going faster and faster in the center of the board. Ashley hung on and sneaked a quick glance at Maya. Her sister's mouth had dropped open and the whites of her eyes showed. Maya was as freaked out by this as she was.

The planchette shot off the board and landed on Maya's bedspread. Ashley stared at her, their hands still hovering above the center of the board.

Maya gasped. "That wasn't supposed to happen, was it? Dad seemed like he was angry or something."

But Leah's words sounded in Ashley's mind. They were supposed to end a session with "Goodbye." They hadn't had a chance to do that. Did the planchette flying off count as a *goodbye*?

A thud on the window made her almost jump out of her skin. Maya froze staring wide-eyed right back at her. "What was that?"

"I don't know." She slipped off the bed, crouching as she tiptoed to the window. Pulling the curtain aside, she looked out at the pine tree across the driveway. Nothing out of the ordinary. And then she looked down to the ground. A black bird with one wing splayed to the side hopped in the small patch of grass like it was trying to fly away. But the way its wing looked was weird. "It was a bird. It must have flown into the window. I think it's hurt."

Maya pounced off the bed and joined her in looking down

at it. "What should we do? Should we try to help it? Take it in to the vet?"

But before Ashley could answer, Lucas stepped out of the house from the kitchen door. He paused seeing the movement in the grass and then he went over. He was directly under them so that they couldn't see the bird. His body jerked and there was a flash of his leg in the dark pants. He bent lower and when he rose he held the bird's leg with the tips of his fingers. It hung limp, swaying with every step he took going across the drive. He pitched it into the trees bordering the property.

"He killed it!"

When he turned he glanced up at their window. They jumped back, but Ashley was sure he had seen them watching. She rose to her tiptoes trying to see what he was doing. He got something out of his car and then went back into the house.

The guy was *such* a creep. And it didn't look like her aunt had broken up with him.

THIRTEEN

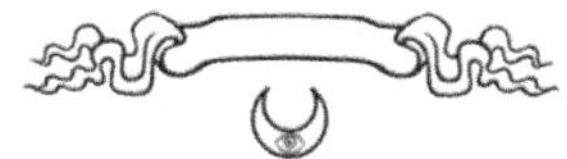

Claire finished setting the plates in the sink and then stood there, her hands gripping the countertop. Either Lucas was lying, or Carol had been seriously mistaken as he'd suggested. Add to that fact that she really disliked him… Well, what he said could be true.

Could be.

She glanced over when he opened the door and came through. His smile was sheepish and his gaze darted past her.

"Got it." He held his phone up and then slipped it into the pocket of the shirt. He kept walking over and placed his hands on her shoulders gently turning her to face him. "I hope you believe me, Claire. Hell, you know how I feel about casinos. I'd rather stick pins in my eyes than hang out there." He grinned. "Maybe I've got a doppelganger in the area. I don't know who Carol saw, but it sure as hell wasn't me."

She looked up examining his eyes. On one hand, it really didn't matter if he'd gone there. It was his life, and he could do what he wanted, go wherever. But it was the lies that were maddening, not to mention *insulting* to her intelligence. And her gut was screaming at her that he was lying.

Maybe it was time to bring this relationship to an end anyway. For the last couple of months things had changed or maybe it was her who had changed.

She looked down. "Look Lucas, we're friends. You don't owe me anything..." Looking up into his eyes again, she continued, "...except that I expect you to be honest with me. If we don't have that, we really don't have anything."

"Jesus, Claire! I'm being honest! I love you!" His grip on her shoulders tightened.

Her chest felt heavy. It wasn't the first time he'd said he loved her but try as she might she couldn't say it back. She'd thought maybe in time she'd grow into that feeling but it was starting to look like that would never happen. What could she expect? She'd jumped into this thing before she even was truly over the divorce from Jake.

"Lucas... I don't know. I think we want different things. You want more and I just can't give it to you, not now." She sighed. "Maybe I never will. And this thing, Carol seeing you at the casino with that woman has brought it all home to me."

He pulled her into his arms, "I wish I could make you see how much you mean to me. I would never do anything to hurt you, like lying or running around. Don't give up on this." He pulled back, and there were tears flooding his eyes.

God. Her stomach dropped down to her knees knowing how much he was hurting. If there was one thing she knew, it was how bad it felt being the one who was dumped. It wasn't that long ago that Jake had done the same thing to her, walking out and ending the marriage. Being the one left behind hurt—a lot!

And talk about honesty. If she was honest with herself, she would have known that her interest in Lucas was a rebound kind of thing. He'd been there when she was vulnerable needing emotional support—dealing with not just her marriage breakdown but the death of her brother and sister-in-law.

Why did life have to be so difficult? Working up her nerve, she looked at him. "I think we need to take a break. It's not forever but for now, we both need to figure out some things."

He shook his head. "No. That's just another way of saying we're breaking up. I don't need to figure anything out. I know what I need and it's you, Claire. You're the first thing I think of when I wake up and the last thing before I go to sleep. Don't do this, Claire. Don't do it to me or you. We'll get past this and make it work."

She faltered a little. "I don't know..." There were things she'd miss. Quiet dinners followed by snuggling watching a movie, talking to another adult about work and stuff. And of course there was the sex, and the fact that he made her feel special and pretty. But was that enough?

Not if she didn't trust him anymore. And she didn't.

He took a deep breath gazing at her with such intensity, "Come over tomorrow night for dinner. Sleep on this and then we can talk. You're tired. This move has taken more out of you that you realize."

Part of her wished that what he said was true. Their relationship had always been comfortable and fun even if she didn't care as much as him. But nothing lasted forever. And this lying was a side to Lucas that was a game changer.

"It's just one night. You owe me that much, Claire."

Her eyes closed and she nodded.

For the first time she knew how hard it had been on Jake leaving her. She huffed a sigh. The irony of it all was that Jake had left because he wanted kids and she didn't. Now she *had* kids. And she wouldn't have it any other way. When Lucas held his arms out to her, she wondered what Jake was doing right then.

Lucas pulled her into him again, rubbing her back. But it didn't help. She felt wooden in his arms.

FOURTEEN

The next day Ashley was just finishing up from her shower and blow-drying her hair when there was a knock on the bathroom door.

Aunt Claire's voice sounded when she turned the dryer off. "Ash? The cable company just called. They are ahead of schedule and can hook the internet and cable up this afternoon."

"Great!" She turned the hair dryer back on, fluffing out her thick mane of damp hair. At least now they could get on the internet, and she could do her own research into the Ouija board. Leah had been fit to be tied when she'd told her what had happened the night before. Now, she wanted to bring crystals and sage and all kinds of things with her when she came over that afternoon. It was a good thing Aunt Claire was going into work to check on things at the office. Who knew what kind of crazy cleansing ceremony that Leah was going to do?

She finished in the bathroom and then went downstairs. Maya was hunched over her bowl of cereal while Claire was tidying up, her hands in a sink full of white suds washing dishes.

She got a bowl down and glanced over at her aunt as she poured the cereal. "A bird flew into Maya's bedroom window last night. It scared the crap out of us."

Aunt Claire looked over at her. "Did it crack the window?"

"No. But it hurt itself. It was on the ground flapping around but its wing looked like it was broken." She looked over at her aunt examining her face. "Lucas saw it and he killed it."

Her aunt's eyes flashed wide. "He killed it? He never mentioned that! It must have been when he went out to the car to get his cell phone. Damn it. That's *horrible*."

"Yeah. We were going to come down to see if we could help it but he just killed it." Ashley's felt her chest fall picturing it. The poor thing. Alive one minute and dead the next because of that brute.

"He must have thought it was going to die anyway. He was just putting it out of its misery, I guess." But Aunt Claire's voice lacked conviction and she seemed sad.

Maya walked over and put her bowl in the sink. "It might have lived if we'd nursed it. Maybe its wing wasn't broken but kind of bruised."

Aunt Claire sighed. "Yeah. But we'll never know, will we?" She changed the subject and smiled. "So the boys are coming out Tuesday? We're getting a raft? I hope the weather holds. Which reminds me. I'll pick up a bunch of water shoes in town."

Ashley looked over from her place at the table. "Will you be home for dinner?"

Claire was quiet for a few beats. "Probably not. I made a casserole for you to heat up. And there's salad stuff in the fridge." Aunt Claire turned and looked at each of them. "Do you think I work too much? I know you spend a lot of time alone and have to fend for yourselves at meals. I could try to cut back if you—"

"We're fine, Aunt Claire. You need the money, and it's not like we're little kids. Even being out here isn't so bad. The lake helps. I mean our friends come out, so it's not like we're really alone. Not like what I thought at first." Ashley could see the pained look in her aunt's eyes. She added, "Plus having the internet will help."

Aunt Claire sighed and looked down at the floor. "I was going to go over to see Lucas after work. But on second thought, I'd rather spend the evening with you. You've been on your own for the last couple of nights, so maybe we'll watch a movie, make some popcorn. How does that sound?"

Maya smiled. "That sounds like a plan."

The sound of a car followed by a banging door brought Ashley to her feet. She peered out the window of the kitchen door. "Leah's here. She's early."

Aunt Claire looked at her watch. "Actually now that she's here, I think I'll go in early too. That way, I might be able to have dinner with you guys. I just want to check on my listings and see what's new."

The knock on the door was followed by Leah striding through with a bulging knapsack over her shoulder. "Hi. My mom had to go to the supermarket to get some things for a bake sale. That's why I'm early. That's okay, right?"

When she stepped away from the door, Preston was in tow. "Hi Maya! Everyone." He looked around at Ashley and Claire. "I wasn't duh...doing anything, suh...so I thought I'd cuh...come out too."

Maya smiled. "I don't think we're allowed to go swimming without the shoes, but we can hang out. I wonder how Henry's doing. Did you talk to him today?"

Preston nodded. "He was pluh...playing a vi...video game. He's n...not doing muh...much. His fuh...foot's sore."

Claire called over her shoulder as she left the room, "If you need anything when I'm gone, just call me. I'm going to have a shower and then head in."

When her footsteps sounded on the stairs and the bathroom door closed, Leah turned to Ashley. "I've got everything we need to fix whatever damage you and Maya did last night."

Ashley felt the muscles in her neck tighten. Sometimes Leah was such a know-it-all. "Everything's okay, I'm sure. But suit yourself."

Leah's eyes went wide and she leaned in. "You're sure, are you? Well you shouldn't have touched the board without me being there! Who knows what—"

"What ha...happened, Maya?" Preston's arm rose cutting his sister off.

Maya threw a dirty look at Leah. "We used the Ouija board. The thingamajig shot off the board when we asked it a question. And then this bird flew into the window and scared the crap outta us."

"See?" Leah scowled and shook her head. "Something like that happened to Allen in my Facebook group. He started seeing this dark specter in his room. And then it kept waking him up in the middle of the night. It was so bad that his family had to call in a priest and have the house blessed. He still swears it's around, following him everywhere."

Ashley felt a cold shudder creep up her back. Holy cow. "Do you think we brought something bad into the house?"

Leah took a deep breath and let it out slowly, "Let's hope not. I just wish you'd listened to me."

Ashley's eyes narrowed. They'd only wanted to contact their parents. "We'll start this when Aunt Claire leaves. Until then, let's go outside."

Maya slumped walking across the room. "I want to see if I can find that bird. We should bury it."

Leah kept up a running monologue as they went out. "Another girl thought she'd reached her grandmother. But the entity attacked her. It left three long scratches on her back. Her family ended up having to move to get away from it."

This was ridiculous. Ashley looked over at Maya who had paused, gaping at Leah. Even Preston looked alarmed, his gaze riveted to his sister. Ashley put her hand on Leah's arm. "Leah. Stop it. We'll fix this and then we won't have anything to worry about."

Leah was not only scaring Maya, but thinking of all the

nights when Claire was working and how isolated they were out there in the country was upsetting.

Maya led the way across the driveway, threading her way through the trees on the other side. Preston stepped into the brush and his leg swung out trying to clear it away to see. "I...I found it."

"Hang on." Ashley darted over to the garden shed at the side of the property. "I'll get a shovel." She yanked the door open and smelled a musty scent of dirt mingling with the smell of gas fumes from the lawn mower. She spotted a shovel propped in the corner and grabbed it, her other hand reaching for her inhaler.

When she went back out, taking a deep haul of the medicine, Maya was walking next to Preston. He held the mangled bird with the tips of his fingers. Its eye was still open but its head had been flattened. Seeing it, made her chest tighten despite the fact she'd just used her inhaler. She nodded to the side of the property and led the way over to a grassy spot.

Leah was right on her heels, "He just stomped on it? I don't think I could ever kill anything. Even if it was to put it out of its misery. I'd never sleep again if I killed anything."

Ashley pushed her foot on the blade of the shovel, slicing through the dirt like it was butter. "Yeah. I know. He's such a jerk. He never hesitated even to check it out before he killed it. It was so fast." She angled the shovel and threw the dirt to the side. After a few more scoops deepened the hole, she said, "That's deep enough. At least this way nothing will get at it." She nodded to Preston who was holding the bird cupped in his hands. He knelt down and dropped it in.

Ashley's gut rolled hearing the thud. She was about to scrape the dirt over it when for some reason, she felt faint. She stumbled to the side and gasped for air. A bead of cold sweat trickled down her temple.

"You okay, Ash?" Maya stepped over and put her hand on Ashley's back.

Ashley swallowed hard, fighting a wave of nausea. It felt

like the cereal she'd eaten was churning in the back of her throat. She passed the shovel to Maya but Preston stepped forward to claim it.

"I'll take that, let me do it." He pushed the loose dirt with the blade covering the dead bird completely. "There." His mouth twitched. "Poor little thing."

Ashley looked over at Leah and saw her own surprise mirrored in her friend's face. But she couldn't say anything, not without embarrassing Preston. It was probably the only time she'd ever heard him speak without the hesitating stutter. He'd actually sounded confident, like Henry.

The kitchen door opened and Claire stepped outside breaking the moment. "I'm off. Help yourself to whatever you want for lunch." She paused seeing them with the shovel, "You buried it? That was a nice thing to do." She opened the door to her car and called out, "See ya later."

Preston stomped on the fresh dirt and then looked over at Ashley. "I'll put the shovel away."

When he was out of earshot, Ashley turned to Leah, "Has he ever spoken that clearly? He didn't stutter at all."

Leah shook her head. "He's been going to a speech therapist for the last three years and never once has he spoken like that. Weird."

Even Maya had noticed. She watched him come back out of the shed. "Yeah. That's weird but good, right?"

"For sure." Leah reached for Ashley's arm and pulled her along to the house. "You look like you could use a glass of water or something. How are you feeling now?"

But as quickly as the sudden sickness had come—it left. "I'm better, but I think I'll drink some water." She looked at Preston and then her forehead furrowed. She'd been sick, and then Preston's stutter had disappeared. Hmm...

When they went inside, she stood at the sink drinking a glass of water and watching Leah root through her knapsack. Leah placed a bundle of dried herbs, a black crystal, and a box of salt on the table. She looked over at Ashley. "I was going to get some holy water too, but Mom hurried me out the door."

Maya went over and picked up the box of salt. "*We've* got salt, Leah. What household doesn't have salt in the pantry?"

Leah snorted. "We're going to use a *lot* of salt Maya. I didn't think your aunt would appreciate us using all of hers."

Preston stepped closer. "Does muh...Mom know y...you have this st...stuff?"

Ashley set the glass in the sink turning away from the look that Leah shot her. So, Preston's change wasn't permanent, just something that happened when they'd buried the bird.

"No! And don't tell her, k?" Leah looked over at Ashley, "Can you get a bowl for me? Just a soup bowl is fine."

When Ashley got it and handed it to her, Leah continued, "We should start in the room where you did the Ouija board. Maya's room, right?" She poured the salt into the bowl and handed it to Maya. "You carry this. We'll need you to put it in the middle of the room." Turning to Preston she added, "You close her bedroom window. We'll seal the room while we cleanse it and then open it again right after."

"You've really researched this, haven't you." It wasn't a question in Ashley's mind. She noticed the amulet that Leah wore when Leah bent to get the bundle of grass and a silver tray for the ashes. It wasn't anything she'd ever seen her friend wear. It was a black stone with a silver wire looping over it.

"You have to know what you're doing when it comes to this stuff, Ash. And that's another thing." Leah looked at each of them in turn. "Don't be scared. Some entities feed off fear. We have to be calm and assured, trusting...no, *knowing* this is going to work. Got it?" Her gray eyes narrowed as she peered at them.

Ashley nodded. "Got it. Are we supposed to pray or say special words?"

Leah picked up the crystal and headed across the kitchen. "Just follow my lead. To be on the safe side, we'll do all the rooms in the house."

Leah looked like anything but a lady oracle in her jean shorts and T-shirt but she was sure acting the part. Ashley looked over at Maya before following her friend up the stairs.

Her sister's eyebrows rose high and then she blew a gush of air softly.

When she entered Maya's room she looked around trying to get a sense or feeling of any presence. But if there was something there, she couldn't sense it.

Preston strained getting the window to slide shut while Maya placed the bowl of salt in the center of her bedroom on the braided rug. Leah fished a lighter from her shorts and lit the bundle of grass. When it caught she grabbed the tray to catch any sparks. Leah let it burn and then blew the flame out leaving the ends smoldering brightly. The scent of the grass was pungent as it drifted in the air.

All three of them stood watching Leah as she walked to the far corner, blowing on the smudge to increase the smoke wafting from it. "I command any entity in the space to leave. By the power of light and goodness, I rebuke you." She continued these words as she wandered to each corner of the room, waving the bundle of grass like she was yielding a sword.

She went to the center of the room and looked at Ashley. "This room is done. Now yours."

Ashley looked up at the hatch covering the entrance to the attic. If they didn't have to go up there it was fine by her. Eew, all that dust and the spider webs. She followed Leah out and into her own room.

She jerked back when she saw the dresser drawer pulled out and pairs of socks on the floor. What the hell? Her heart pounded fast as she crept over to peek inside. The Ouija board rested in the bottom drawer.

Her eyes widened and she turned to Maya. "Did you put the Ouija board in my room?" Maya shook her head, gaping at the board.

It was a shot in the dark but she had to ask, "Do you think Aunt Claire did this?"

"Maybe?" This time it was Maya who was grasping at straws, but there was fear in her eyes.

Leah's head turned from looking at the board and her face was set in a frown. "I think we'll have to take our time in here.

If you didn't move it and Maya didn't move it..."

Ashley's gaze roamed over her room from the bright green bedspread to the desk and her dresser. Oh God. She would give anything right about then for it to have been her aunt who moved it, even if it meant she'd be in trouble. Had the thing moved itself or some entity—

The doorbell rang and she jumped.

Her hand went to her chest and she breathed a fast sigh. "I'd better get it. It's got to be the cable guy."

Leah gripped her arm before Ashley had a chance to get out of the room. "This isn't good, Ashley. Close the door after you. We'll be a while in here."

Ashley felt a mixture of relief and guilt as she raced down the stairs. She's left them up there to deal with whatever was in that room. But if she'd been there she'd just be standing there watching Leah do her spell or chant or whatever. Plus, they needed someone there to tell the cable guy where to string the wire. Shit.

It *had* to be Aunt Claire who'd moved the board. Either that or Maya was playing tricks on her. Yeah. That had to be it.

She wished they'd never found that blasted board.

FIFTEEN

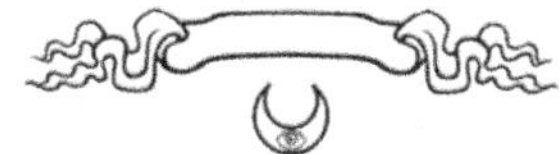

It was probably the tenth time that Ashley wandered from the living room to the staircase looking up, listening hard while the cable guy worked in the living room. Leah's voice was a soft, muffled sound, still working in her bedroom to cleanse it.

When the cable guy spoke next to her ear, she skittered sideways before clasping the newel post. Her heart was in her throat and she gasped.

He smiled. "Sorry to startle you. I've done the work inside. Now I've just got to install the dish and get it aligned." His eyes narrowed watching her. "You okay, miss?"

She nodded. "Yeah. I've got friends over, and I want to get back to what we were doing. Do you need me down here anymore?"

"No. Go ahead. I'll leave the invoice in the mailbox." With that he went out the door, the tools on his equipment belt clamoring with each step.

Ashley raced up the stairs and hesitated for just a beat before entering her bedroom. God! They'd been up there for almost fifteen minutes! The room was a haze of smoke but she could see Leah standing in the center of the room. The bundle of brush was burned about halfway from its original size.

"You can open the window, Preston."

Ashley stepped closer and gripped his arm. "Better not. If a cloud of smoke goes out the opening the cable guy might think the house is on fire."

Leah nodded. "Good point."

"Well? Do you think it worked?" Ashley's stomach was a knot when she looked at Leah. She noticed that the dresser drawer was closed.

"I think so. But just in case I poured a line of salt along each wall. Salt is really good for repelling spirits. I don't know why but everyone says it works. How about we do the rest of the house?" Leah stepped over to the door waiting for Ashley to open it, since she still held the bundle and tray for the ashes.

As Maya stepped by her carrying the bowl, she leaned in. "That was weird about the board, huh?"

Ashley examined her sister's face for any twitch of a grin. But her sister was serious. So, if she hadn't done it, it had to be Aunt Claire. She held Maya's arm. "Is it still in the drawer?"

"Yeah." Maya stepped out into the hallway.

"So...th...the cable i...is hooked uh...up?" Preston's voice was calm, asking about the cable as if the ritual they'd just done was nothing to be worked up about.

Ashley turned to look back at him as they crossed the hallway to her aunt's room. "Yeah. I think so. Preston, did you feel weird when you were covering up that bird?"

"A...a little. Whu...why?"

"Just curious, that's all." She turned and followed Maya into Aunt Claire's bedroom. She looked around feeling like some kind of intruder. There was her aunt's bed all made up, her night table with the book she was reading still open to where she'd left it. There was a shelf with more books next to the window. The photo album she'd seen when they were moving in was set up as a bookend.

Leah jerked her head, indicating the window, when Preston entered. "This room won't take long. But we've got to do it just in case."

Maya set the bowl down. "I hope she doesn't smell this when she gets home."

Leah started walking over to the corner, next to the closet. "We'll air everything out. She won't know." She blew on the smudge and once more began the incantation, "I command any spirit to leave this place. By the power of light and goodness, I rebuke you."

Ashley had heard it so many times she could say it in her sleep. But she kept silent, watching her friend complete the task.

When they were finished the room and even the bathroom, walking down the stairs, Maya asked, "Now that the house is just about cleansed of any evil spirit, I can still do the board to contact Mom and Dad, right?"

Ashley turned on her. "Are you crazy? We should get rid of that thing. We're not sure that Aunt Claire moved that board, Maya! But we sure as hell know that *something* did!"

Leah stepped off the bottom step. "We cleansed the house, Ash. Whatever was here playing a trick is gone."

"So you say! I think we should get rid of that board. This isn't healthy doing this." Ashley looked over at Maya. "Let Mom and Dad be, Maya. You can't bring them back."

But Maya's mouth was a straight line and her eyes flinty when she stared back at her sister. "You're not the boss of me. If I want to contact them again, I will."

Ashley looked over at Leah for support. Leah sighed but her eyes sparked. "Only do it if I'm there, Maya! Do you want to have to go through this every time you use the board?"

It was all Ashley could do to keep from yelling at both of them. "You're as bad as she is, Leah! She wants to contact our parents, but you...you just eat this stuff up like its candy!" She turned to Preston, her last hope, "What do you think?"

His face colored pink and then he looked at Maya. "I th...think ih...if she wuh...wants to u...use it with Le...Leah, she can."

Ashley ground her teeth so hard they crackled. Of course

she should have known Preston would side with Maya. "Maya, leave this alone. I'm not telling you to, I'm asking. This isn't something you want to pursue. Let. It. Go."

"You let it go! First you think it's all BS and then you're scared of it. Which is it, Ash?" Maya stormed off to the living room and there was a plunk as she set the bowl of salt down.

Leah turned to her. "I'll watch her. It'll be all right, Ash."

She hissed her answer, "But you're not here all the time, Leah. What then?"

Leah shrugged. "Lock it up. Get a lock on your dresser drawer if you think she's gonna use it without me. Actually that's probably a good idea anyway."

Her chin led the way getting in Leah's face. "A better thing is to just burn it or throw it in the trash."

But Leah only smiled. "Calm down, Ashley. It'll be fine. I'll look after everything. I'm fixing your mess now, aren't I?"

Ashley's arms clenched over her chest as she watched Leah and Preston follow Maya. For two cents she'd go back upstairs and break the damned board. She plopped down onto the bottom step. There was one thing she could do. She could tell Aunt Claire.

She sighed. Who was she kidding? She wouldn't rat her sister out and also risk getting Leah into trouble. No. She'd have to go along and make sure Maya never played with the board on her own.

SIXTEEN

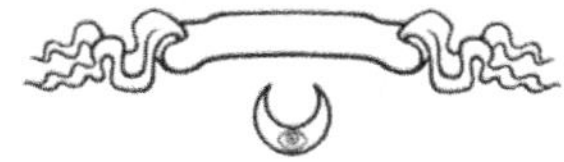

It was an hour later over a lunch of soup and sandwiches that Leah looked over at Ashley. "So? Were you ever going to mention the party on Tuesday to me? If anyone has a right to be pissed it's me, Ash. Mason Sherwood is coming over and you were going to hog him all to yourself?"

Ashley's eyes widened and she sputtered, "I didn't get the chance. Not with all your voodoo shit." Part of her had wanted to stay silent on the Mason raft-building thing, but she should have known that Preston would tell his sister.

"Huh!" Leah picked up her empty bowl and plate and brushed Ashley's shoulder with her hip on the way by. "Well, I know now, don't I? And that voodoo shit as you call it saved your ass, didn't it?"

Maya looked over at Preston. "I'd like to give the board another try this afternoon while Aunt Claire is away."

Ashley's eyes narrowed. Well, *that* didn't take long.

Leah looked over at Ashley when she spoke, "This time let's set up the white candle I brought. It's supposed to be helpful in only getting good spirits to come. Like your parents."

Maya jumped to her feet and grabbed her things to take to the sink. "C'mon Preston. We'll get it set up."

The look in her eyes all excited shot a jolt of pain through Ashley's heart. Maya was still trying to deal with the death of their parents and if this was the only way that helped, who was she to stop her? Besides which, she probably would sneak off to do it alone. And that wouldn't be good.

She took the rest of the things from the table and watched as Preston rose to follow Maya. He'd even worn what looked like a brand new T-shirt and shorts, and his hair was smooth like he'd put some gel or mousse on it. The kid was going all out to impress her, even taking advantage of Henry's injury to be with her and score points.

Ashley yelled after them when she heard their footsteps on the stairs, "Wait for us, Maya! Don't you start this on your own!"

Leah turned to her and her gaze was even. "I'll watch her, Ashley. Plus, it helped her with the guilt...you know, what she said to your mother that night."

Ashley nodded, "Maybe. But I'm not sure about any of this. That Ouija board in my dresser. That freaks me out, Leah."

Leah put her arm over Ashley's shoulder. "We fixed the problem, Ash. From now on, maybe you'll listen to me with all my voodoo shit, huh?"

Ashley slumped and led the way across the kitchen. "I can't believe I'm doing this again." She trudged up the stairs and then into her room. Leah was right behind her with a spring in her footsteps.

When they got to the room, Maya had pulled the curtain and had the board set on the floor between her and Preston. She looked up. "See? We waited." She looked over at Preston. "What should we ask Mom?"

"Muh...maybe make shu...sure it's her fir...first, okay?"

Ashley sat next to her sister and sat Indian style on the rug. "He's got a point. Especially after what happened." She looked over at Leah. "If you sense something else is taking over with the planchette, we stop immediately, right?"

"Absolutely." Leah placed her fingertips on the board and looked at each of them. "Ready?" When all of them had their left hand on the reader she began, "Are there any spirits here with us? We seek benign spirits only. Robert or Gail Vincent. Are you present?"

The reader began to move, just a little at first toward the "Yes." Ashley glanced over at Maya and saw her eyes lit up.

"Ask if they can see the future," Maya whispered.

Leah shook her head. "Where they are is timeless and they can see everything. But they're not allowed to tell us. Try something else."

Preston whispered, "Ah...ask them suh...something that only thu...they would kn...know to muh...make sure it's thu...them."

Leah nodded. "That's a good point. Especially after what happened."

Maya thought for a moment. "If it's Mom, what was your grandmother's name?"

"You don't know the name? How will you know if what they say is true?" Ashley peered at her sister.

"It's in the family Bible. I saw it on Claire's bookshelf earlier. We can check it and see."

Leah shrugged and then asked, "Tell us the name of your grandmother."

Ashley watched the planchette. It moved a little and then hesitated going in small circles. She held her breath wondering if this was going to be a repeat of what had happened the night before. But the reader slid over to the letter "P" and quicker this time it slid to "E," "A," "R" and then to the "L."

Maya looked over at her. "Pearl?"

Ashley got to her feet. "Before you do any more let me check this." She raced from the room and over to Claire's. She grabbed the old, black-leather tome and then thumbed through to find it. It was there! A family tree with six layers of branches. Her eyes stung looking at her mother's handwriting with her name and Maya's. But three branches above it with another hand was written Pearl Elmsley nee Garrett.

She set the book back on the shelf and raced back. It was her. Pearl was an odd name, old-fashioned. When she entered the room they all looked up at her. "It's true." She took her place beside Maya and placed her fingertips on the reader.

"Mom? I miss you." Maya's voice was a faint whisper. "Do you miss us?"

The planchette began to circle the board and then it hovered over the letter "H." Ashley looked over at Leah. "What's it doing?"

Leah's eyes were wide. "I think she's got a message for us." She swallowed hard and then resumed, "Do you wish to tell us something?"

The planchette swooped to the letter "E," "L" and then when it reached the "P," it stopped.

"Help? You want to help us?"

The planchette shot to the "No."

Leah sat back and let out a gush of air before continuing, "Help *you*?"

The planchette shot to the "Yes" so fast it was hard to keep her fingers connected.

Preston leaned close to Maya. "Ask her to spell out what she wants."

Leah and Ashley shared a look. He'd done it again—spoken without the stutter.

"What is it you wish from us?" Maya leaned closer to the board.

The planchette shot to the letters "F," "A," "I," "R" and then to the "Y." Ashley's fingers tingled as she tried to keep them on the reader. Fairy? "What is she getting at?"

Preston looked over. "I've got a feeling I know what's next."

The planchette scraped across the board to the "C," "I," "R," back to the "C" and then the last two letters before stopping—fairy circle.

"I knew it." Preston looked around at the others. He gazed at the planchette. "What about the fairy circle?"

Ashley's breath froze in her chest as she waited for the

board to answer. None of this was making any sense. She watched as the planchette once more began to move. It stopped at "B," "O," "D" and then paused on the 'Y' before starting small circles around the letter. Body. Fairy circle body.

She looked over at Maya. "What's that got to do with Mom?"

Leah spoke, "Is this still Gail Vincent?"

Ashley felt a chill raise the hackles of her arm. She was ready for this to stop but still she kept her fingers on the reader. She gasped as it shot to the word "No" in the far right corner. That was it! Enough. She pulled her hand back.

But Leah wasn't stopping. "What is your name?"

The reader circled fast like it was getting impatient or something. Then it shot to the "S," "K," "Y," "L," "A" and came to an abrupt stop on the "R."

"Skylar?" In answer to Leah's question it shot to the "Yes" word.

Preston spoke again, "What about the fairy circle, Skylar? You said body. Is your body there or near there?"

The planchette shot away from the "Yes" and then back to it.

Ashley had heard enough. And a glance at Maya told her that her sister was frozen with fear. "We should stop. Put it on "Goodbye," Leah."

But Leah shook her head. "We need to find out more. If there was a body there in the fairy circle wouldn't we have seen a grave marker or a fresh pile of dirt if it was recent?"

But the reader wasn't through yet. Ashley watched with horror as the object continued the message, "K," "I," "L," "L," "E" and ended with "R."

"Enough! Put this board away!"

Leah knew enough not to argue with her shouted words. She pulled the planchette to the "Goodbye."

Maya pulled her hand back and looked over at Ashley. "That was creepy."

Preston blew out a long sigh. "Yu...yeah."

Ashley's gaze flew to him and then Leah. Preston didn't

even seem to notice that his speech had changed during the session. But Maya had. She peered at Preston.

Leah blew out the candle that was set on the bedside table beside her. "I don't think we reached a bad spirit. She's asking for our help. Maybe we're the only ones who can give her any peace. Should we go back there?"

Ashley thought of the crazy woman running at her from her yard. Mrs. Kovac. There was no way she wanted to go by her house again—not if she could help it.

"Yu...you have the ih...internet now. Wuh...why not start thu...there?"

Ashley looked at Preston. "Yeah. Skylar's not that common a name. Let's do a search for anyone with that name."

SEVENTEEN

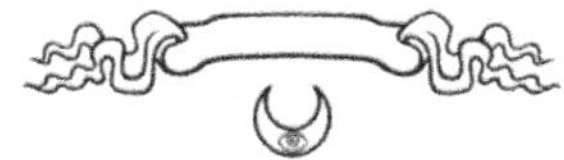

Ashley sat at the kitchen table with her laptop while Leah perched like a vulture next to her. Across from them, Maya and Preston were scanning Maya's tablet.

Maya looked over. "Wow. It feels like forever since I've been online."

Ashley rolled her eyes. "It was only three days, Maya. Give it a rest." She typed the words "Skylar" and "Saranac Lake" into the search bar and hit enter. "Huh. There's a couple Skylars here on Facebook." She kept scrolling while Leah pulled out her cell phone.

"Speaking of Facebook, I should update the group on what just happened. Maybe someone else had an experience like this." Her thumbs flew on the tiny keyboard.

Ashley noticed the web page change to headings centered on the location, Saranac. She clicked on the Facebook link of the first Skylar. It showed a bunch of pictures of a young girl and her dog. The person had posted a comment today so that couldn't be it.

The Skylar they'd contacted was dead and had spelled out the word "killer." She looked over at Preston and Maya. "If

Skylar was murdered and her body is somewhere near that fairy circle, shouldn't we let the police know?"

Leah snorted. "And tell them what? That we contacted a spirit? And the spirit said their body is in a fairy circle? They'd think we're crazy kids. And maybe they'd tell my mom about what we've been doing. I still think we should go back there. We may have more luck than trying to find anything on the internet."

Preston looked up from the tablet. "Muh...maybe there's suh...something on the shu...sheriff's office wuh...website. A mi...missing person."

"Yeah! Good thinking Preston!" Maya smiled and then went back to using the tablet. She yelped, jerking back as her glass of pop tipped and then smashed on the floor. "Shit!"

Ashley looked at the dark stain covering Maya's shorts, "You spilled your pop?" She rose to her feet. "Be careful, clumsy."

Maya stared at Preston who shook his head. "I...I didn't duh...do it."

Maya rolled her eyes. "Well, I didn't!" She got up from the table stepping carefully to avoid the shards of glass on the floor. "I've got to go change out of these wet clothes."

Leah looked over at her brother. "Don't move till we get that glass cleared away." She got up and joined Ashley who was grabbing the roll of paper towels to sop the mess up.

They had just cleaned it up and were on their way back to the trashcan under the sink to dump the garbage when a scream upstairs pierced the air. Ashley froze for a second.

Maya.

Ashley dropped the wet towels and raced across the room. She took the stairs two at a time; her friends' footsteps behind her barely registering. When she got to Maya's bedroom, her sister stood in the center of the room trembling. The whites of her eyes showed, and she darted over to Ashley.

"What happened?" Ashley held her sister close, rubbing her back. She eased away to look closely at her.

"I saw her!" Maya's eyes flooded with tears, and her face

had blanched of all color.

The hair on the back of Ashley's neck spiked, and a shudder rippled through her shoulders. "Who, Maya? Who or what did you see?"

Maya spun and she pointed at the window. "She was there! It was a young woman. She was staring at me from the window when I came in to get changed."

Ashley stared at the window. They were on the second floor. "Maya, that's not possible. Are you sure you saw a face?"

Leah stepped forward and her hand rested on Maya's shoulder. "What did she look like?"

Maya sobbed while her hands rubbed the tops of her arms, closing in on herself. "She had blond hair but her eyes...Oh God. There was only black where her eyes should have been!"

It was Preston who went over to the window looking out. When he turned, he looked at Maya. "There's nothing out there." He went over to her and pulled her into a hug.

Ashley's heart pounded like a racehorse and she gulped air. She grabbed her inhaler from her pocket and took a long breath of the medicine.

Leah looked at each of them. "It was her. This Skylar girl. It had to be! Oh my God. I can't wait to post this to the group."

Ashley took another deep breath and went over to stand next to Maya. She stroked her head and then spoke, "You're sure you saw a face? Could it have been a trick of the light? Some kind of weird reflection like the sun coming out from behind a cloud?"

"No," Maya squeaked out between sobs. "It was a face. It was horrible. She looked angry."

Ashley spun around glaring at Leah. "You said it would be fine in here. Well it isn't fine, Leah. Fix this! Do whatever it takes. Maya is scared to death because of that stupid Ouija board. That's it! I'm throwing it in the trash."

She stomped out of the room ignoring Leah's protests. This was Leah's fault for wanting to use the board in the first place. Her and her stupid Facebook group! She yanked the bottom drawer out and grabbed the board. She debated whether to burn it in the fire pit or just take it out to the shed and tuck it into the garbage.

When she passed by the room and saw Maya crying, still being comforted by Preston, she made up her mind. Maya needed her. Burning it would take too long. As long as it was out of the house they'd be okay.

She passed Leah coming up the stairs with her knapsack and the bowl of salt. For once she had the sensitivity to look ashamed, barely meeting her eyes. And so she should be!

The screen door banged behind her and she marched over to the shed. She lifted the lid of the gray metal container and shoved the board deep into the bag of trash. Good riddance.

She raced back to the house, looking up briefly at Maya's bedroom window and then to the pine across the driveway. With the sun still so high overhead it didn't seem possible that it could have caused a shadow creating an illusion in the window.

No. As much as she hated to admit it, Maya had seen a ghost.

She sprinted up the stairs and then stood for a moment gasping for air. When she felt calmer she walked into Maya's bedroom. Already, threads of smoke from the burning bundle in Leah's hand drifted in the air.

"Maya?" She walked over and pulled at Maya's hand leading her from the room and shutting the door.

"It's okay, Maya. Leah will fix this and the board is gone." She led Maya to the bathroom. "Have a shower and I'll bring you some clean clothes. When you get dressed, it will all be over. No need to worry about it."

Maya's eyes were bleary when she looked at Ashley, "Why couldn't it have been Mom I saw? Why that girl?"

Ashley's heart broke looking at her little sister. "I don't know. But you won't see her again. I promise." She tried to sound confident even if she didn't entirely feel that way.

And as much as she knew Leah would be angry, she had to tell Aunt Claire about this.

***

Ten minutes later Ashley leaned against the bathroom door waiting for her sister. Leah and Preston were still in Maya's room and she could hear the muffled chant from across the hall. She stood straighter, hearing the hiss of the shower stop. "Maya? Are you okay?"

"Yeah. I'm fine now."

Ashley let out a long sigh of relief. When Maya's door opened and Leah stepped out, Ashley glared at her. "Are you finished? Did it work?"

Leah sighed. "I think so." Her eyes closed for a moment. "No. I know so." When she spoke again, she kind of flinched, "I'm sorry, Ash. This is my fault."

Ashley's resolve softened a little watching her friend. She could tell that Leah really regretted this. "I shouldn't have gone along with it. It's my fault too."

Preston stepped out and glanced at the closed door of the bathroom. "Is Muh...Maya all right?"

Before Ashley had a chance to answer the door behind her opened and Maya slipped out. She had on a pair of capri pants and a cotton shirt and her damp hair hung in wet strands over her shoulders. She looked at each of them. "I'm okay now, I think." She looked at Leah. "Is it gone? Will it come back?"

Ashley lifted a lock of hair from her sister's cheek and tucked it behind her ear. "You can sleep with me tonight. Nothing bad is gonna happen to you, not with me there."

"Did you get rid of the board?" Leah winced bringing it up. She hung on to the strap of her knapsack on her shoulder like it was a lifeline.

"Yes. I put it in the bottom of the trash bag in case Aunt Claire would see it when she throws any garbage in." Ashley's shoulders squared. "But I think I have to tell her about this."

Leah was shaking her head the moment Ashley brought up telling. "No. Please don't tell her. It's over and we can forget about all this. She might tell my mother and then I'll be grounded. I might not be able to see you again."

Preston's eyes widened as her words sunk in. "Nuh...no. Muh...maybe we can fi...fix this."

Ashley gaped at him. "Fix it? Some girl is dead and now she's somehow latched on to us to help her? With any luck she won't be back to scare the hell out of Maya or me but we have to tell Aunt Claire. She might know someone at the police department, someone she sold a house to, that she could ask about this Skylar girl."

Maya added, "We could ask her to not tell your mom. Aunt Claire is nice. She wouldn't want you to get in trouble and not be allowed to see us."

Leah looked like she wasn't entirely convinced. "This Skylar needs our help. If we can find her body, she'll have peace and leave us alone. Can you just put off telling your aunt for one day? Give us a chance to try to solve this mystery on our own? I really don't want my mother finding out."

Ashley didn't feel right about not telling Claire but she also hated to get Leah and Preston in trouble at home. She looked at Leah. "Are you staying over tonight? I'll wait one day but only if you're here. Just in case..." Her gaze flitted to Maya.

"Absolutely! I brought my PJs. I knew you'd ask me to stay." She looked over at Preston. "Mom's picking you up at five. You'd better act normal and keep quiet about this."

"Ca...can I tuh...tell Henry?"

"I don't care. He was here the first night we used the Ouija board so he's okay, I guess." Leah turned to Maya. "I'll even sleep on the floor so you can have the spot next to Ash. With the two of us with you, there'll be no worries."

Preston made for the stairs. "I'm guh...going to keep looking on the ih...internet. Muh...maybe we'll find out more. A...about thi...this Skylar."

Leah followed him, and she looked over her shoulder at Ashley. "I'm going to post this to the group. There are a few people who have experience with ghosts. Maybe I'll pick up something." She stopped with her foot on the stair. "But you know...if we went to the fairy circle we could nose around. We wouldn't have to step inside it."

Ashley's eyebrows rose. "The old bat down the road scares me more than that circle. That's a last resort. But if we can't find out anything today or tonight, we need to go back there. With Aunt Claire."

Her cell phone buzzed and she pulled it out of her pocket. When she saw the name come up, she smiled. Oooh! Mason Sherwood! She read the message,

"Looking forward to a day at your place. We're still on, right?"

Her chest lightened. He hadn't said *it's* still on. He'd written *We're* still on.

She held back from the others who were going down the stairs. Leaning against the railing she typed a reply.

"Can't wait. Absolutely, we're still on. Pray for sunshine."

She peered at the "pray for sunshine." Did she sound too eager with that? She backspaced the cursor, erasing it.

"Hope for sunshine."

She smiled and followed the others.

This time they settled in the living room without any drinks when they did their research. Ashley searched the police website and found nothing. She kept clicking and found a website that dealt with missing persons. There was a national registry. God. Who knew so many people went missing? She typed in the first name "Skylar."

Leah looked over at her. "Hey! There's this girl in the group who went through a true haunting. She just joined. It's pretty creepy what she went through."

Ashley scowled at her. "I hope you aren't putting our real names on this site."

Leah affected a deep voice, "The names have been changed to protect the innocent." She grinned. "I'm not totally crazy, Ash. It *is* the internet."

EIGHTEEN

Claire hung up the phone and closed her eyes. Lucas's words rang in her ear—he was disappointed and hurt that she was canceling their evening. She'd thought about breaking it off when she called, but she couldn't do it with a phone call. She would, the next time she saw him. But hopefully that could wait a few days. Maybe he'd start to realize that it was over and it would be easier.

The negatives of staying in a relationship with him had tipped when he'd lied to her about being at the casino. And when the girls had told her about him killing that bird, the final penny dropped. He hadn't even thought enough about killing something to mention it? That was just *cold.*

At the tap on her office door she looked up. Gerry filled the opening with his squat and rotund body. There was a small sheepish smile on his face. "Can you do a favor for me?"

Uh oh. But he was her boss, so she forced a smile. "Sure. What's up?"

He let out a long sigh and he slumped lower. "I scheduled an open house at the Mountain Estates tomorrow evening, six to nine. I forgot it's my wedding anniversary. If I don't take

Marjorie out for dinner, I'll be in the doghouse for a month. Can you cover for me?"

Tomorrow the girls had asked Mason and the gang out to build that raft and then have a BBQ. She had wanted to be there. Shit. Trust Gerry to screw up his dates. She stood up. "Of course. No problem."

"Thanks Claire. I owe you." Gerry gave the doorframe another quick tap and smiled. "I hope you sell it; I even put an ad in the paper for the open house." He turned around and left whistling a tune.

Well, it wasn't like she had to be at the girls' BBQ to chaperone. Hell, there were enough kids to do that. And she could have everything set up before she left anyway. She put her listing book and tablet in her case and was just about out the door when her cell phone buzzed with a text. She paused and pulled it from her purse. It was probably the girls wanting her to pick something up something on her way home.

Her brow furrowed seeing Carol's name pop up on the screen. She read:

"Hey, remember that hooker I saw with Lucas? I just saw a poster with her picture on it. She's missing."

Claire's eyes narrowed as she typed.

"Maybe she met a sugar daddy and left for bigger places. Speaking of Lucas...I'm breaking it off with him."

Her chest slumped with the weight of what she'd written. Now it was official and she couldn't put it off much longer. She'd miss some things about him. But the relationship had gone past its "best before" date.

She smiled seeing Carol's answer pop up.

"About time! There's plenty of fish in the sea. You hooked up with him too soon after the divorce. IMO."

"Yeah. I think so too in hindsight. 20/20, right? Gotta go. Spending evening with girls—movie night."

"They'll love that. Have fun."

Claire put her phone away and left the office. As she drove from the small town to her new home she thought about what Carol had written—that girl going missing. And Lucas. But surely in that lifestyle, hustling in a casino, there was no permanence. The girl could be in Miami by now sipping a margarita by some rich, old man's pool.

As she got closer to her house, she noticed a beige sedan pulling out of her driveway. She peered at it as it passed by and waved seeing Preston and his mother. Ruth Mitchell barely managed a smile waving back. The woman was the original "Church Lady" off *Saturday Night Live* from back when she was just a kid. She'd seen enough You Tube videos to know Ruth could put Dana Carvey to shame.

When she got out of the car she reached for the bag of water shoes and popcorn she'd picked up at the discount store. There was an assortment of colors and sizes for anyone who might stop by for a swim.

When she went into the house it was quiet. "Maya? Ashley?" She set the bag down and smiled seeing that they'd done the dishes and everything was tidy.

They were in the living room glued to their screens. It wasn't hard to tell that the cable guy had been out and they were connected. "Earth to Maya! Earth to Ashley, Leah. Hello?"

They looked up and as one they said "hi" before going back to their screens. But, in that fleeting glance she could tell that something had happened.

They looked...guilty.

NINETEEN

Ashley set the laptop aside and went out to the kitchen. Her aunt was pulling the tags off the items she'd bought and looked up when she entered. Ashley wandered over, "These shoes will do the trick."

Claire smiled. "Yeah, and they were cheap. What'd you girls do today?"

Ashley hesitated for a moment picking up a blue pair of shoes and examining them. She tried to keep her voice casual, "Not much. Been surfing the web since the cable got hooked up."

With a glance to the doorway Claire's voice was lower, "So, Leah is staying the night? I don't mind it's just that I thought an evening with just us hanging out would be fun. We don't do it all that much."

Ashley shrugged, even though after what had happened earlier in the day she was happy to have Leah there. "Sorry. But we're just watching a movie anyway."

Claire peered at her closely. "Everything all right, Ash? You seem kind of quiet. Were you and Maya arguing?"

Ashley's eyes opened wide and the words rushed out. "No. Everything's fine." She had to change the subject before she blurted it out. There were still some second thoughts about telling her aunt.

"I'm thinking of tomorrow when Mason and everyone's out to work on that raft. I hope the weather holds is all. It's been nice all week so we're probably due for rain."

"I think we're going to be good with that. I heard a forecast on the radio on the way home." Claire's smile fell. "But I'll miss the BBQ. Gerry screwed up and I have to cover for him at the model home. I'll be here most of the day though."

"That's good." Ashley stammered, "I mean good you'll be here, not because you have to work in the evening. You'll miss our bonfire."

Her aunt gave her that puzzled look again but before she had a chance to say anything more, Maya and Leah came into the kitchen. Ashley looked at her sister for any sign that her earlier fright was evident. Aunt Claire was sharp and would be sure to pick up on it.

"Look at all the shoes Aunt Claire bought, Maya! She has enough for an army." She scooped up a purple pair that looked like Maya's size. "Try these."

Even Leah was giving her weird looks with how animated she was over water shoes. But Aunt Claire was suspicious and this might be a useful distraction. Maya wandered over and took the shoes.

She tried them on and then looked over at her aunt. "You got my size in my favorite color. Thanks." Maya's voice held all the excitement of going to a funeral.

Ashley scowled at her sister. Maya could at least try to sound more normal.

Leah must have picked up on her aunt's questioning look because she piped up, "I hope it's okay for me to stay tonight. If you want to go get changed or sit and have a glass of wine, I'll help Ashley get dinner on." She looked over at Maya. "Why don't you find a movie on Netflix for tonight?"

Aunt Claire's gaze flitted between Leah and Ashley. "Sure. I'll get a glass and then join Maya. I thought a comedy might be nice."

Ashley caught Maya's eye and gave her a look. When her sister passed by she whispered, "Act normal."

Leah had the glass of wine poured and handed it to Aunt Claire. "Here you go!"

Aunt Claire smiled but it didn't extend to her eyes. She shot a look at Ashley before following Maya into the living room.

Leah rushed over as soon as they were gone. "She's gonna blow this! I know she's still kind of creeped out but she's got to keep that to herself. If your aunt finds out, I'm toast."

"I know. But what can we do? We'll just have to trust her to keep quiet." She looked away for a moment. "I'm pretty sure Aunt Claire wouldn't say anything to your mom." From the odd comment that Claire had made about Ruth Mitchell, she wasn't a big fan. But Leah didn't have to know that.

"*Pretty sure* doesn't cut it, Ash." Leah got the casserole out of the fridge and turned the oven on. "Once we're settled with the movie, things will be fine. It's getting through dinner that might be tricky."

***

Three hours later with the Melissa McCarthy movie winding down, Ashley glanced over at her aunt. Dinner *had* been tricky but she'd managed to keep the subject on Claire's favorite interest, the renovations. Even Maya had perked up after a few kicks to her shins under the table.

But Aunt Claire had also been kind of quiet, like she was preoccupied or something. When Leah had asked about Lucas, her aunt had changed the subject. It looked like they weren't the only ones keeping a few secrets.

When the movie ended, Aunt Claire rose and stretched her arms to the ceiling. She was still grinning from the movie when she looked down at them. "If you want to go on up, I'll clear up here. I want to take the garbage bag out to the shed and then I'll lock up."

Ashley's eyes flared wider. The Ouija board was in the big trash can in the shed! She picked up the empty bowl where the popcorn had been and rose to her feet. "I'll get the trash out, Aunt Claire. You worked today. If you want to go on up, I can look after the lights and lock up."

Aunt Claire's smile fell, replaced by another puzzled look. "You're sure? You don't usually do that."

Ashley's eyebrows rose. "I'm fifteen, Aunt Claire. I need to do more around here to help you out." She walked across the room calling over her shoulder, "Besides, I really don't mind."

Leah was right on her heels. "I'll keep you company. It's pitch-black out there."

"C'mon Maya! Looks like we're off the hook." Her aunt's voice drifted in from the other room and was soon followed by their footsteps on the stairs.

Ashley turned to Leah, gripping her arm. "Maybe you should have gone up with Maya. Check her room in case...well you know."

Leah's mouth fell open and she raced after them. "Wait for me! Changed my mind. If there's a skunk or raccoon out there, Ashley's on her own."

Great. Aunt Claire would surely wonder now. Nice going, Leah.

Ashley grabbed the bag of trash from under the sink and slipped her cell phone from her pocket. She turned on the flashlight app and then went out the door. There was a reason she never did this chore, especially at night. The light over the door only lit an arc of the driveway and she was soon out of its beam. The sounds of crickets and the rustle of leaves in the trees were the only sound besides the gravel crunching under her feet.

She pushed the door of the shed open and shone the light down on the floor to see her way. She was about to reach for the lid of the large garbage can but froze.

Oh my God. The Ouija board was set up on top of the can! The planchette was resting on the word "No."

Tossing the bag inside, her heart beat fast as she raced back to the house. When she was inside, she flipped the dead bolt and then leaned back against the wooden door. Gulping air, she took the inhaler out and took a deep breath of it. Oh my God! That board had been just sitting there...waiting.

For her.

TWENTY

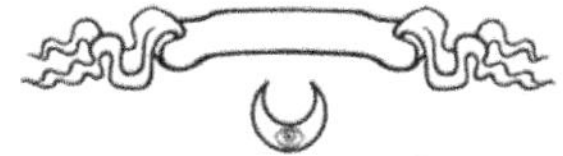

It took a long time to catch her breath and calm down enough to lock the other doors. Ashley walked slowly up the stairs. The only sound was her footsteps. No screams from Maya or Leah. No. The horror had been waiting for *her,* outside in the dark.

Her hands rubbed her upper arms when she paused at the top step looking over at her aunt's bedroom. Aunt Claire was still up from the crease of light showing along the floor under the door. It was so tempting to go in and tell her what had happened.

She took a deep breath and squared her shoulders. No. She'd talk to Leah about it and then decide whether to let her aunt know. But this was seriously creepy. As creepy as finding that damned Ouija board in her drawer. And the planchette resting on the word "No" had been a message—she wasn't getting rid of it that easily. Damnit! Why hadn't she burned it that afternoon?

She hurried down the hall and entered her bedroom. Maya was tucked in on the far side of her bed while Leah was curled up in a sleeping bag on the carpet.

Leah sat up. "What's wrong? You look like you've seen a… a—"

"Don't say it!" Ashley looked over at Maya. The poor kid had been through enough of a scare that day. This was going to put her over the edge. She made a decision seeing the fear in her sister's eyes. "It was dark and creepy out there. I hate the dark and then there's those animals lurking in the woods."

Leah sank down into the cocoon of her bed. "You volunteered. What'd you expect?"

Ashley had to bite down on the inside of her cheek to keep from lashing out at Leah. This was her fault. And she's said she'd fixed this mess. Well it was far from being fixed by the looks of it. She pulled the comforter back and got in beside her sister, not even bothering to put her PJs on.

"Aunt Claire suspects something, doesn't she?" Maya plumped the pillow under her head and looked over at her.

"Yes. She's not stupid. But this is gonna stop tomorrow. I've decided to burn that Ouija board. I want to see the ashes and know it's gone for good."

Maya whispered, "We'll put it in the bonfire. Aunt Claire will be gone and she'll never know about any of this." Her eyes fell. "But that girl, Skylar. What are we gonna do about her? We have to go to the fairy circle, Ash. Maybe Mason will drive us so we don't have to be anywhere near that old woman."

Leah strained up on her elbow. "He's got a truck. There's not room for all of us. I know what I'm doing with that circle so I'd better go with him."

It was the proverbial straw for Ashley. She hissed down at her friend, "He's got room in the back of it for everyone. But it'll be me riding shotgun up front, Leah. Not you."

Leah reached up and turned the bedside lamp off. "You don't have to be so pissy about it, Ash." Her words were followed by a sniff and the sound of her getting comfortable on the floor.

Pretty soon the sounds of their breathing, slow and regular told Ashley that Maya and Leah were asleep. But sleep would be a long time coming to claim her.

***

When she woke the next morning Maya and Leah were gone. She grabbed her cell phone and looked at the time. Ten after ten!

She threw the covers back and stepped over to the window to peer out. There were some clouds on the horizon but the sun was shining on the water. The weather was good so far for the day they had planned.

As she walked across the room her chest tightened. That damned Ouija board.

She'd been so scared that she'd left it sitting on the garbage can. If Aunt Claire went in there to get something she'd find it! Shit! Her eyes narrowed. She wasn't going to do that alone though. Leah was going to help her hide it till they could toss it in the fire pit.

When she stepped out of the room, she noticed the bathroom door shut and the hiss of the shower spray. Great. She had to go and someone was hogging the bathroom.

She clomped down the stairs feeling like she hadn't slept a wink all night. The only sleep had been filled with bad dreams, and all centered around that blasted board. Aunt Claire was sitting at the table with a coffee, scanning her laptop. She looked up when Ashley entered, "Good morning! I thought you'd be up at the crack of dawn getting dolled up for your company."

"I slept like shit."

"Language! That's too bad. You'll perk up soon." Aunt Claire went back to her reading.

"When are they coming out?" Maya put her plate in the sink and turned to Ashley. "I wonder if Henry's foot is better. I want to go swimming with him and Preston too."

"I don't know. Probably after lunch." Ashley scowled and looked up at the ceiling. "Great. She's gonna be in there for hours primping, and I gotta use the bathroom."

"Go to the one down here." Claire gave Ashley a dirty look. "Someone is pretty crabby this morning."

"Fine! But I wanted to have a shower too!" Ashley stomped

across the room.

"Did you sleep in your clothes?"

But Ashley was too pissed to answer her aunt. She went into the bathroom that doubled as a laundry room and went about her business, all the while fuming. She finished up and then when she was washing her hands, she paused. True she had slept like hell but even so, to be this out of sorts was weird.

It wasn't even Leah she was angry with. Everyone and everything was straining her last nerve. It was that damned Ouija board. It had to be.

She took a deep breath and forced a smile going into the kitchen to get something to eat. "You were right about the weather, Aunt Claire. It might rain but not until tonight. Not from the looks of the sky."

"Enough time for your—" Claire's cell phone beeped and her words trailed off as she read the text message. "Shit. This is an out of town client. He's going to be at the office in an hour." She closed her laptop and rose to her feet. As she carried the empty mug to the sink she continued, "It's the second time he wants to see the house on Maple, so I think he's going to buy it."

Ashley stared at her aunt. "So you have to work?" She popped two slices of bread in the toaster and noticed the gleam in her aunt's eyes. She always got fired up when she sold a house.

"Sorry. But it pays the mortgage." Aunt Claire walked across the kitchen and paused in the doorway. "I gotta get changed. The hamburger is thawed, and all you have to do is make patties. You'll be fine. Just save me one, will ya?"

Ashley had to smile at her. When she was excited like this she looked like a teenager, more like an older sister than her aunt. Her long hair pulled up into a ponytail and the yoga pants ending at her knees with the oversized T-shirt helped with that as well.

Leah passed her on the stairs and then came into the kitchen. "So your aunt has to work, huh?" She opened the fridge and took out the jug of milk pouring a glass. "You sure slept in. I thought you were never going to get out of bed."

Ashley couldn't resist. "I thought you'd never finish in the shower!" It came out more harshly than she'd intended.

Maya shot her a look and then said, "I'm going to play some MineCraft. Let me know when you need my help getting the food ready." She left, heading across the hall to the living room.

Ashley stepped over to Leah and grasped her arm. "You won't believe what happened last night!"

Leah's eyes popped. "What?"

"That damned board was set up on top of the garbage can when I went outside! The reader was on "No" like it was telling me we can't get rid of it! I almost had a heart attack! I didn't want to tell you with Maya listening."

Leah's mouth had fallen open as Ashley talked. She closed it and swallowed hard. "Oh shit. This is not good." Her step faltered, and she placed her other hand on Ashley's arm. "Oh boy."

"You're telling me! I meant it Leah when I said I'm gonna burn it." Ashley glared at her friend. "Don't say anything to Maya. She's scared enough. But after Aunt Claire goes, you've gotta do that cleansing thing again, even though I'm not sure how much it will help."

"I think you're right about burning it." Leah looked down at the floor and her eyes narrowed. "I've got to post this to the group. Maybe I missed something in the cleansing ritual. This shouldn't have happened."

"Do what you have to do." Ashley shook her head in frustration. "We have to hide that stupid board in case Maya or Claire go in the shed and see it. I'm not touching it though. I've *had* it with that thing."

"Okay. I'll do it." Leah pulled the stone of the necklace she wore out and her fingers closed over it. "I've got this to protect me at least. "

Ashley pulled at Leah's fingers. "What is that?"

"Tourmaline. It's supposed to keep evil spirits away."

"Well, maybe it's working. You didn't see a ghost like Maya did. And twice I found that creepy board moved from where I'd left it." She led the way across the kitchen and out the door. "You're definitely the one who's gonna move it."

She looked over her shoulder making sure that Claire nor Maya wasn't following before she darted across the driveway and opened the door of the shed. Her hand flew to her neck, and she almost fell stumbling backward.

"What?" Leah stepped past her and looked in the shed.

"It's gone again." The hair on her arms spiked high.

"You're sure it was there last night?"

"Yeah. I swear it was even set up!" Her heart raced and it was hard to breathe, let alone get those words out.

Leah gripped Ashley's shoulders giving her a shake. "Maybe your aunt took it. She was up before us. She could have went in the shed and found it. Maybe she threw it back in the can."

Ashley could feel her chest tighten even more. She grabbed her inhaler and then after a long puff, she looked at her friend. "You check the can if you like but I'm not. Leah, this thing is evil. It's not in there. God only knows where it's going to show up next."

Leah crept into the shed and lifted the lid from the trash can. She poked around, moving a few small kitchen bags and then covered it again. When she turned she had paled and her eyes were wide. "It's not there. You're right."

TWENTY ONE

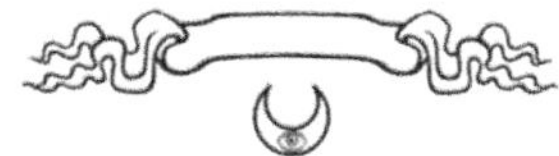

Ashley had the kitchen door open, about to enter when her aunt stepped out.

"What's wrong?" Aunt Claire's worried gaze flitted from Ashley to Leah. "What were you two doing? You look like you've seen a—"

"Don't say it." Ashley took a deep breath squaring her shoulders. "We were just putting some stuff in the garbage."

"Didn't you do that last night?"

"Yeah. But I didn't get it all. And I wasn't sure I had closed the door when I left it. Don't want a raccoon to get in there and making a mess." Ashley could feel her face getting warm. For sure she didn't look pale now. God, she hated this lying and sneaking around.

"There's something more to this. But I don't have time right now to get into it. I'll probably be late as it is." Aunt Claire walked past them on her way to the car. She held the car door open and her face was tight when she spoke, "We'll talk when I get home. Leah, maybe you should stick around and spend the night. You're in on this too, whatever it is."

She got in her car and backed out of the driveway.

Ashley turned to Leah. "I should have told her everything. Now, I'm going to be in trouble for lying too."

Leah sighed. "We're goners. And so is the board. Shit."

Ashley's phone buzzed and she took it out of her pocket. When she saw who it was her eyes went wide. "It's Mason. They'll be here in an hour." She looked over at Leah. "Shit! I haven't even showered!"

"Go ahead. Maya and I can handle making the food. It's just burgers."

Ashley hightailed it into the house and up the stairs. The creepy board and the upcoming shit-storm that her aunt was going to lay on her was still there but she didn't have to face that for a little while. She stepped into the bathroom and checked that her robe was there before peeling her clothes off.

As she turned the shower on, her gut sank thinking of that girl, Skylar. Here she was getting ready for sort of a party, and that girl was dead. And what's more, they couldn't put off the trip to that fairy clearing to look for her body. She said a quick prayer that they wouldn't find anything. It would be waaay too horrible if they did.

***

When she went down the stairs, the sounds of Maya and Leah working in the kitchen was a dull backdrop to the music blaring through the house. Ashley smiled. The shower, fresh clothes and her new perfume had helped a lot in lifting her spirits. Or was it the fact that Mason would be arriving any minute?

Leah was hidden behind the open refrigerator door while Maya sprinted across the kitchen yelling, "They're here!"

Ashley smiled when Leah moved so fast that she bumped her head on a shelf in the refrigerator before closing it. "Eager much, Leah?"

Leah smirked. "Look who's talking! Is that a new top? I haven't seen that one before. And look who's even wearing lipstick."

"Shush! They're just outside. You're one to criticize, Leah.

I've never seen that green blouse on you before!" Before Leah could reply, she added, "Let's go say hi." Ashley walked over to the door not even caring that Leah shoved past her to get out first. They had all afternoon. Plus, she was still wondering how to bring up the subject of the Ouija board and the spooky stuff without Mason thinking they were crazy.

Mason was the first one she looked at, the muscles in his arms gleaming as he unloaded the lumber and barrels. He glanced over at her and smiled. "Hi Ashley. Great day for this!" He looked at Leah. "Do you *live* here? Every time I visit, you're here."

Leah ignored the snide comment and smiled. "Can you blame me? With the lake and—"

"Get my tool box will ya, Preston?" Mason kept piling the boards.

Ashley saw Preston hop up into the truck bed while Henry was standing chatting to Maya. She called over to him, "How's the foot, Henry?"

"It's better. Staying off it a day helped, I think." He went back to talking to her sister.

Leah stepped closer to Mason. "Need a hand taking this closer to the lake?" She shielded her eyes with her hand gazing up at him.

"Yeah. Sure. I guess that makes more sense to build it there. Less distance to carry it when it's done." He looked over at Ashley. "So your aunt had to work today?"

She laughed and went over to help Leah with the heavy board. "Yeah. That might be a good thing for Leah and me."

He straightened, hooking his thumbs in the back pockets of his jeans as he gazed at her. "Oh yeah? How come?"

Ashley glanced over to her sister, but Maya and Henry were walking toward the lake out of earshot. "We're in a bit of trouble with Aunt Claire."

He grinned. "What'd you do? Run your cell phone bill up?"

She sighed and started walking slowly with the end of the board. She was about to answer but Leah beat her to it.

"We found a Ouija board and used it."

He looked at Ashley when he spoke, "You don't really believe in that stuff, do you?" He fell into step beside her, carrying a barrel and leaving Leah trailing with the end of the board in her hands.

She felt her neck grow warm when she looked over at him. "I didn't at first but now...I believe. Too many creepy things have happened for it not to be real."

Leah wasn't going to be shunted aside so easily. She actually gushed, "We used it to contact their parents. We made sure it was them but then this girl's spirit came through. Skylar is her name. She told us where her body is."

Mason stopped dead in his tracks. "Ashley. I don't really believe in this stuff but I don't think you should scare yourselves like this. I mean you're out here on your own a lot with your aunt's job."

"Believe me, I wish I hadn't laid eyes on that board." She was about to say more but Leah again jumped in.

"We kept the board in Maya's dresser but then it moved to Ashley's room, all on its own. It totally freaked us out but that was nothing compared to what Ashley saw last night."

He peered at her, and his hand rose to rest on her arm. "What happened last night?"

For a moment all she could focus on was the intensity of his gaze, but then her brain kicked in. "We couldn't let Aunt Claire know about this because of Leah's mom. She'd be in serious trouble if she knew. You know how she is with religion and church stuff."

He glanced back at Leah. "Yeah, I guess, but go on."

"I put the board in the trash can in the shed. Real deep in case Aunt Claire would come in and see it. When I went out last night with a bag of garbage, the board was set up on the lid of the trash can." Just thinking of it made her chest hitch and she reached for her inhaler.

"Do you think maybe Maya went out and did that? Pranking you?"

She shook her head. "Maya saw the dead girl's face in her bedroom window. On the second floor."

He looked up at the house and his brow furrowed. "So she's scared too? Doesn't sound like she'd play a trick, feeling like that." He looked back at her. "So where is this board now? I'll get rid of it for you."

Again, Leah jumped in, "That's just it! It's gone! We looked this morning but it wasn't there."

Preston had been following them, lugging the heavy toolbox. "Wuh...what? It was guh...gone? Where is ih...it now?"

Leah turned and hissed at him, "You can't tell Maya, Preston. She was freaked out yesterday about that face in the window. She'll really freak about this."

"I wuh...won't."

Ashley blew out a sigh and looked over at Mason. "Can I ask you for a favor?"

"Building you a raft isn't enough? You want more?" He grinned to let her know he was teasing. "Sure. What do you need? As long as it's not a million dollars, you've got it."

"Only a few hundred thousand dollars. Can you manage that?" She chuckled. It felt like forever since she'd laughed. "Actually, I need you to take me to the spot where this girl said her body is located."

"Is it in Alaska? Please tell me I don't have to drive you there." There was that cute glint in his smiling eyes when he looked at her.

"Hey you guys! This isn't a joking matter, y'know!"

Ashley turned to look at her friend, wondering if the chastisement had more to do with Mason flirting with her, and leaving Leah out. "You're right. This is actually sad." She turned back to Mason. "It's actually just down the road a couple of miles."

Mason blinked a couple of times looking at her and Leah. "And you couldn't do this on your own? Don't get me wrong, I'll take you but..."

Ashley swallowed hard, knowing how this probably sounded to him. And the next part was going to put her squarely into Kooksville. "There's a crazy, old woman who lives down the road. She ran at us when we biked by."

"Sh...she was real scuh...scary, man. A wih...witch."

Uh oh. From the way Mason looked at Preston he was totally convinced they were crazy, if not juvenile. Especially since he was seventeen. But when he looked over at Ashley he smiled. "Look. If it will help you get past this, show you there's nothing there but your overactive imaginations, I'll do it."

"Buh...but the board, man. Huh...how did it juh...just disappear?"

Mason rolled his eyes and grinned at Preston. "The crazy lady, or witch, or whatever she is, came over and took it. That has to be it if Ashley's aunt didn't find it first."

They continued over to where Maya and Henry were standing at the shore. Leah turned to Mason. "If you want to go take a look, I can show you the spot where the Ouija board said her body is."

Maya shot a look at Ashley. "We're going to the fairy circle now? You convinced Mason to take us?"

Ashley winced knowing that fairy circle had to be the icing on the kooky-cake for Mason. "Yeah. We might as well get it over with. You don't have to come though."

Henry grinned at his brother. "Oh man. You'd better watch your step if you go near that circle. Leah has a conniption if you step inside it. I can't wait to see this."

Mason peered at Leah and she flared red to the roots of her blond hair. Her chin rose high. "It's a sacred spot. It's bad luck to go inside the circle. You'll see when you get there."

Ashley felt sorry for Leah being so centered out, especially when Mason had made a few snide remarks directed at her.

Leah sneered at Henry. "Odd, how you made fun of it and then your foot was sliced open afterward."

Mason's fingers threaded through his hair for a moment as he stood quietly looking at the ground. Ashley held her breath watching him deliberate. Finally he spoke, "Okay. But if we're looking for a body or grave we *all* go. That way, we can cover more ground." He glanced at Leah. "...Sacred or otherwise."

"Thanks Mason. I know how this sounds. I hope we don't find anything, but we've got to look, just in case."

Maya added to Ashley's words, "Mason, I saw her face in my window. I wish I hadn't but I really did. She wasn't old or anything, just scary. She was *killed,* Mason."

He smirked. "Why do I feel like I just landed in a Nancy Drew novel? We'll get this over with and then you guys will have to let this go. Seriously. You're scaring yourselves over nothing."

When Henry, Preston, and Maya were settled, sitting on their butts in the back of the truck, Mason lifted the tailgate up, slamming it shut. "Stay put and hang on. This isn't exactly legal y'know."

Ashley opened the passenger door and got in. For once Leah didn't try to insert herself next to Mason. When Leah got in, Ashley turned to her. "I'll try to keep them out of that circle. I know you think it's important."

But Leah sniffed and looked out the side window. Ashley's chest fell as she looked at the back of Leah's head. She'd try to make it up to her somehow.

When Mason got in and started the truck, Ashley looked out the windshield at the sky. A steel-gray cloud skimmed over the sun, casting a pall on the bright day.

They pulled onto the road and Ashley spoke, "You must have seen the crazy, old woman around town. She's the one who talks to herself in a foreign language. Aunt Claire says her name is Mrs. Kovac. She's Romanian or something."

"That's who's got you freaked out?" Mason's eyebrows rose when he looked at Ashley. "She's odd, but pretty harmless I'd guess."

"Not when she runs at you and almost knocks you off the bike!" When they passed the bend in the road, she pointed at the old cottage up ahead. "That's her house."

"Looks pretty rundown."

The old lady was sitting in a rocker on her front porch as they passed by. She held a cat in her arms and started to rise from the chair. Ashley turned to look and saw the woman pointing at them. She couldn't hear what she yelled but even if she had, it would probably be in that strange language anyway.

Leah turned to Mason. "It's just up ahead on the left. You can see a path where the fence is broken."

"Okay. I see it." Mason flipped his signal on and pulled off the road, parking the truck. "This is it, right?"

Ashley closed her eyes and nodded. "Yeah." She took a deep breath. "This is it."

TWENTY TWO

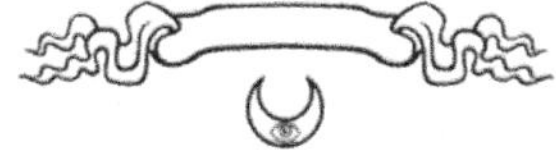

Leah led the way following the path through the forest. Ashley walked more slowly, scanning the underbrush on each side for any sign that someone had been through there. But everything looked lush and undisturbed, without a broken branch or even a crushed leaf.

"We're here." Leah came to a halt at the edge of the clearing.

Ashley looked over at the dark green grass blowing slightly in the breeze that now felt cool on her skin. The others crowded around looking at the strange circle surrounded by thick trees.

Mason spoke in a hushed voice, "It *is* kind of weird." He waved his hands before him. "The air…it just feels strange, man…almost like water or something." He scanned the grass before them, his head turning from side to side. "And… I think that's a perfect circle, you know that?"

"Told ya," said Leah.

"Okay, it's weird; I'll grant you that." Mason's arm reached out, taking in the circle before them. "But it hasn't been disturbed. If we're going to find anything it won't be in there."

Leah looked at each of them in turn. "Let's treat this circle like it's a clock with that birch over there being twelve. I'll take the twelve to two section to search, widening back to cover fifty feet or so. Preston, you take the two to four section and Maya the four to six." She started winding her way through the trees on the edge of the circle. Waving her hand behind her, she said, "The rest of you can figure out what you want to cover."

Maya looked over at Ashley. There was no need for words. They both knew Leah was pissed off.

Mason watched her leave and then he spoke, "Sounds like a good plan." He turned to Henry. "You take six to eight. I'll cover eight to ten and then Ashley you take ten to midnight." He looked up at the sky. "We'd better hurry though. It looks like it may pour any minute."

Ashley followed Leah and looking at the clearing she made an assessment of where to start. The underbrush scratched her bare legs as she swung her feet out stepping along, inspecting the ground for any sign of the dead girl. Even a scrap of cloth. God. She hoped she or Maya wouldn't be the ones to find anything horrible, like a bone or skull.

She swatted a mosquito that landed on her forearm and then waved her hands clearing the swarm. She could see Leah's red shirt through the thicket of trees about twenty feet away.

"I'm getting eaten alive, man!" Henry shouted.

"Quit complaining!" Maya countered from her spot across the way.

Ashley double backed sweeping the area a few feet out from where she'd started. The first raindrop fell on her neck and rolled down her spine. She looked up but the canopy of branches and leaves hid most of the sky. She moved quicker, searching more with her eyes and protecting her bare legs.

Another cold raindrop was followed by more and more. She shivered and held her upper arms in her hands, rubbing them.

"It's raining!"

"No shit, Sherlock!"

She sighed hearing Maya and Henry's banter. That was before the sky opened up and sent them scurrying out of the forest toward the path. A clap of thunder felt like a tremor going through Ashley's bones.

"Hurry!" Mason stood on the path with water dripping from his outstretched fingers.

She raced by him, feeling the sodden ground squish with every step. She could hear Leah right behind her while Maya, Preston, and Henry were a blur ahead, sprinting through the downpour.

When they got to the truck Henry was climbing onto the back, cursing that they had to ride in the open. This time it was Preston who answered him, "Shut up. Quit com...complaining."

Ashley yanked the door open and clambered inside, pushing over to make room for Leah. "Holy cow! That came up fast."

A streak of lightening cut through the bank of clouds, flashing as it arced to the earth. Ashley counted the seconds. She only got to two before the clap of thunder shook the truck. "It's right over us."

Mason got in after securing the truck's back gate. He was soaking wet, the water dripping off his hair that was plastered to his head. "Where the hell did that come from so fast?" He looked over at Leah and smiled. "And no hocus-pocus out of you, Leah, about that fairy circle."

Leah pushed a wet strand of hair from her cheek and sniffed. "Just a storm. We were due for one anyway." She pinched the edges of her green blouse and fluttered it, shaking water off. "I'm drenched!"

Ashley stared at her for a second. There was something strange about Leah's top, but she couldn't put her finger on it. Before she could say or think anything else, the truck lurched as Mason cut the wheel.

Mason managed to turn the truck around even though the downpour was milky, making it hard to see the sides of the road. He drove slowly and glanced in the rearview mirror.

"Those poor kids. They look like drowned rats."

Ashley squinted peering at the road ahead. For just a moment it looked like there was someone standing there. The windshield wipers were a fast metronome with the space cleared quickly blurring again with water. But it was there again. Just a glimpse but enough to know it was someone standing in the center of the road!

"Stop!" Her hand shot out to grip Mason's arm. "There's someone there!"

Mason hit the brakes but they still shot forward caught on a sheet of water. Ashley jerked back waiting for the impact but the truck came to a stop. There in the center of the road was the old woman. She walked to the passenger side and her hand with fingers splayed banged on the window.

Ashley's heart pumped fast against her ribs. "Drive. Let's get out of here!"

But it was too late. Leah had pressed the button to lower the glass. The old lady stared at Ashley. Her dark eyes were flinty framed in the worn lines of her face.

Her lips pulled back, revealing small sharp teeth. "You!" She glared at Leah. "What have you done?"

Mason gaped at her. "They haven't done anything! What's wrong with you, standing out in the rain like this? I could have hit you. Step back. We've gotta get home." He pressed the button on his side and the window rose shutting the old crone off.

As he pressed the accelerator he looked over at Ashley, "Okay. I can see why she freaked you out. She's seriously crazy. I could have hit her with the truck in this storm."

Ashley ignored him and looked at Leah. "She knows about the Ouija board and what we've done. That day she came out after me. I think she was trying to warn me."

TWENTY THREE

It was a mad dash for the house when the truck pulled in. Maya and the others hopped over the side of the bed before they were fully stopped.

When they got inside, water pooled on the floor around Maya and the boys. Ashley looked over at them. "Stay here. I think there's a load of towels in the dryer." She toed her sneakers off and raced to the back of the house.

When she returned, Mason was standing at the kitchen window looking out at the lake. "I'm not sure this is going to clear up." He turned and looked over at her. "That old woman...thank God you saw her in time."

Leah wiped her face with the towel Ashley handed to her and spoke, "Yeah. She must have really wanted to talk to us coming out in this weather."

"She's crazy. Isn't that what crazy people do?" Henry sneered and went back to drying his hair. He looked at Maya. "Can I put my clothes in the dryer?" He put his hand against his cheek. "Maybe I should get in the dryer with them? I'm totally soaked!"

"Sure. I'll lend you and Preston some sweat pants and

shirts. I've got a pretty pink set just for you, Henry." Maya smiled before leaving the room.

"I'm not wearing pink." Henry nudged Preston's arm. "That's your color, bud. It'll look good with your pretty blue eyes."

"Nuh...no way."

Ashley looked over at Mason. "I don't have anything that'll fit you. Unless you want to wear my bathrobe."

Mason sighed and stepped over to his brother. "Maybe we should get going."

A piercing scream from above filled the house. Maya's voice following in a shattering screech, "ASHLEY!"

Ashley tore across the room ignoring Leah's words behind her, "Oh God. What now? Shit! I never did the cleansing."

She bounded up the stairs and gasped standing in the doorway of Maya's room. Her sister's fingers covered her cheeks, and her eyes were rimmed in white as she stood in the center of her room. Ashley's jaw fell open. It was like a cyclone had touched down in there! Every drawer in her dresser was pulled out. Clothes were strewn over the floor and the bed. Even the closet was open, the clothes bar now empty with only a few hangers.

"What the hell?" Mason walked into the room looking around at the mess.

Henry went over to Maya. "What happened in here? You redecorating or something?"

"Not funny Henry!" she snapped.

"Ih...it's still here." Preston turned and looked at his sister. "You wuh...were supposed tuh...to have fi...fixed this."

"I didn't, Preston. I was going to do it again but I never got the chance." Leah stepped over to Maya and rubbed her back. "Get whatever clothes you need and go downstairs."

Henry shook his head. "No problem finding them. They're all on display."

Mason turned to Ashley. "I'll help you. But we were only gone for about an hour—if that! Do you think someone came into the house and did this?" He answered his own question,

"That doesn't make sense. To just break in and wreck one room. Nothing is missing is it, Maya?"

Maya burst into tears and yelled, "It's that stupid board and that girl! She did this!"

If she wrecked Maya's room then...Ashley broke away from the group and raced down the hall to her own room. Her mouth fell open seeing it. Everything was pitched helter-skelter around the room. Even the curtain rod hung down from one side. "She did it here too!"

Leah stood behind her looking over her shoulder at the mayhem. "This is creepy. Nothing was upset downstairs. Just your rooms."

Mason came up and pushed past them, stepping into the room. "Do you think maybe that old woman came in while we were gone? She had enough time and you didn't lock the door. Just like she moved the Ouija board. That's got to be it."

Maya called from across the stairwell, "Aunt Claire's room wasn't touched."

Ashley breathed a sigh of relief for that small blessing at least. Ignoring Mason she turned to Leah. "You mentioned that you hadn't brought holy water yesterday. Maybe it didn't take—the ritual I mean—without it."

Preston came up behind his sister and looked up at Ashley. "We guh...got what wuh...we need. We'll tuh...take Maya downstairs and sih...sit with her."

"Thanks, Preston. Don't leave her alone for a minute, okay?" She looked back at Leah. "The holy water, Leah. Did you need it for this to work?"

"Maybe. I don't *know*." Leah pulled her bottom lip in, biting down at it as she looked around the room.

"Well—find out! Go online and ask in that group you belong to! We need help with this!" Ashley was on the verge of tears. They couldn't live like this with some spirit or entity scaring the hell out of them. And if not for Leah they never would have played around with that board! Wherever the hell it had gone!

Mason had been watching the exchange between Ashley

and Leah. He looked at Leah. "I'll help Ashley tidy the two rooms. You go do whatever it is she wants you to do." When Leah left, he said, "I'm glad I didn't just drop you off and leave. I'm going to stick around until your aunt gets home."

She looked up and the concern in his eyes melted her resolve not to cry. Tears flowed as she murmured, "Thanks."

He pulled her into his arms, rubbing her back with his hands. "It'll be okay Ashley. You'll get through this."

She wasn't sure she had the strength to get through anything like this. Looking up at him she sniffed. "It started so innocently. We wanted to contact my parents. We did...or I thought we did. Now I'm not sure."

"Ashley, you're strong. But you need a shoulder to lean on right now. I'm that shoulder." He smiled and stroked her hair. "But it's a cold shoulder I'm afraid. I'll take you up on that offer of your robe, if the offer 's still open."

"Pink? Like Henry's?" She managed a small smile.

He leaned in and kissed her forehead. "See? That's the spirit. Told you you're strong." He leaned down and grabbed her white terry robe that was draped over her rug. "Not pink though. I'll just be in the bathroom across the hall. You get changed out of those wet things too."

Ashley closed the door after him. When she turned, she shuddered looking around the room. They had used the Ouija board in her room and in Maya's. The two rooms which were attacked. That was no coincidence.

She peeled the wet clothes from her body and grabbed the first things she saw to throw on—jeans and a T-shirt. Opening the door to set the wet clothes outside, she saw Mason emerge from the bathroom. She had to smile seeing him in her robe. It ended just above his knees and there was a red rose embroidered on each pocket over his hips.

He smiled and then did a vamp walk down the hall toward her, primping his hair with his fingertips. "Modeling the latest creation by Jackie Chang is Mason Sherwood."

"It's Vera Wang, you nut!" She couldn't help laughing at his antics. He was trying to make the best of a horrifying nightmare, making her smile.

"Jackie Chang works for me, Ash. And speaking of work..." He slipped by her and began picking up the clothes.

Ashley swooped ahead of him, grabbing her undies and shoving them into the top drawer of the dresser. She rolled her eyes. Here she was picking up after some ghost attacked and thinking of her privacy. Crazy.

"And you thought you'd be doing something fun like building a raft. Ha!" She paused setting the lampshade back on the bedside light. "Seriously Mason. If Leah can't fix this, I don't know what I'm gonna do. I can't go on like this."

He looked over at her and sighed. "If you're right, and I'm not entirely convinced you are, there has to be another solution. Maybe even getting a priest to visit to bless the house. I've seen enough horror movies to know that."

Ashley sank down onto her bed. "That means Aunt Claire will know. Leah's mother will know. But it might be the only way."

"What's worse? Getting grounded for a week or continually cleaning up after a ghost. I'd take the grounding in a heartbeat." He grabbed her hand and pulled her to her feet. "C'mon slacker. We've still got Maya's mess to clean up."

A clap of thunder made Ashley jump as she walked after him to the other room. "Let's hurry and get downstairs. I want to check Maya and see what Leah found out, if anything."

"If you want to go ahead, I'll finish up here. Don't forget the wet clothes though. With any luck mine will be dry by the time I finish. Henry will never live it down...me prancing around in a girl's bathrobe."

She grabbed the clothes and then smiled as she walked past him. "Don't forget he's decked out in pink."

"Take a pic, will ya?" He laughed as he went into the room.

Ashley checked the clothes in the dryer and pulled them out, tossing hers and Mason's in afterward. She went back to the kitchen and saw Maya sitting at the table, bordered by both boys. Maya looked up. "Is it all cleaned up?"

"Mason is doing your room. I wanted to see how *you're*

doing." She went over and rubbed her hand on Maya's shoulder.

Her sister's eyes welled with tears. "I want to call Aunt Claire. We've got to tell her everything, Ash."

Ashley looked at Preston. He'd be sure to catch hell at home as well as Leah. But he nodded his agreement with Maya. She took a deep breath watching her sister. Maybe Maya was right. This was turning out to be way bigger than they could handle.

Leah came bounding into the kitchen. Her eyes were lit up and she actually grinned. "I've got it, Ashley! I talked to this girl out west. She had an actual run-in with a demon! Crazy huh? She threw salt at it and it worked! You've got to read her story. Honestly."

Ashley hardly dared to hold out hope. She held her voice even when she spoke, "What's a demon got to do with this, Leah? This is a troubled spirit. This Skylar girl is trying to get our attention."

Maya murmured, "She's got mine all right."

Henry chirped. "Well, I want to see her too—is she good-looking?" Everyone stopped and stared at him. "What?"

Leah threw her head back. "Shut up, Henry." She blew out a long exasperated sigh. "Salt. We didn't use enough! Don't you see? We need to cover every opening and leave it there. You swept up what we left yesterday so your aunt wouldn't see. But we can't do that. We need to leave it and even leave a bowl of it in the room."

Ashley blinked looking at her friend. "That's it? I can't believe it can be that simple, Leah."

They all jumped at the sound of a yelp from upstairs. Mason's footsteps raced down the stairs and he ran over to where they were standing. His face was as white as the robe he wore. "I saw something! That thing you saw, Maya! A girl's face was in the window staring at me!" He panted, his voice breaking in fear gulping air while the whites of his eyes showed.

Henry popped to his feet. "Seriously? I gotta see—"

"No!" Mason grabbed his brother's arm. "No way! You're not going up there, kid. She looked mad and scary as hell."

He turned to Ashley and Leah. "I didn't believe you. Not until I saw that face! This is for real! Shit!"

Leah's eyes narrowed. "Scared now, Mason? You thought we were crazy. *Now* you believe us!"

Crash! The whole house shook! Again, Mason yelped.

"Thu...that came from upstairs." Preston grabbed Maya's arm.

Ashley raced across the kitchen and stood at the bottom of the stairs peering up. But there was nothing to be seen. It could have been a tree limb coming down in the storm but she had her doubts.

Leah and Mason came out of the kitchen to stand beside her looking up the stairs. Mason whispered, "We should check it out."

But Leah shook her head. "Let me get my things first. We need protection."

Mason gave Leah a funny look but then he nodded. "Yeah. Protection." He turned to Ashley. "Do you have a gun?"

Ashley grabbed her inhaler to take a deep breath, not caring that Mason saw her do that anymore. Her heart was hammering fast and she felt like she'd faint at any minute, if not have a heart attack! She shook her head, willing her heart to slow. Finally she was able to get the words out. "No. But a gun's not gonna help anyway if it's a ghost."

"I'm calling Aunt Claire!" Maya stood in the doorway of the kitchen with her cell phone in her hand.

"Just give it a minute, Maya!" Leah pleaded with her eyes looking at Maya. "Give me a chance to fix this. And if I can't, call her then. Twenty minutes. That's all I'm asking for. You're safe down here. The bad shit is up there."

Preston and Henry appeared at Maya's side, walking her back to the kitchen.

Leah raced to the living room and came back with her backpack. Digging into it, she handed the salt to Ashley and the crystal to Mason before flicking the lighter on the bundle of grass.

"What's that? How is this gonna work?" Mason looked at the crystal and pulled a face sniffing the burning bundle.

"Never mind. Just do what I say. I'll go first." Leah led the way leaving a trail of smoke behind her as she walked slowly up the stairs. "By the power of God, I command you to leave."

Ashley noticed she had changed it up a little, now mentioning God by name. Calling on the big guns for help now. Maybe that was good? She followed her friend and began the chant herself.

"Oh man," Mason said, "this is too much."

Ashley threw a scowl at him. "Just shut up and say it. This has *got* to work." Now was not the time to be a smart-ass.

"Okay, okay. By the power of God I command you to leave." He glared at her. "Happy?"

But Ashley was too intent on saying the words, peering around to see...what? A ghost? Please God, no. The storm had made everything dim with dark shadows crouching in the corners.

Leah didn't hesitate going in Maya's room. She kept waving the wand of dried grass before her continuing her chant. Ashley flicked the light switch and held her breath, waiting for something to happen, but nothing did. Other than the room still being a holy mess, nothing was tipped over that could have made that crash.

"Put salt by the window, Ash," Leah said.

She walked to the window and poured a thick line of salt along the ledge. She continued along all the walls until she got to the doorway.

Leah waved the wand and turned to Ashley. "Leave a heap in the center of the floor. We forgot the bowl but it doesn't matter."

Ashley made a small mound and then followed Leah and Mason out the door. She poured a thick line across the opening. "Leave us in peace." She straightened and her gut fell knowing the crash could only have come from her room and it was next.

Leah stood in the opening of Ashley's room and her head turned, her eyes wide peering at Ashley. "Your dresser. That's what we heard."

Ashley crept forward peeking over Leah's shoulder. Her face tightened seeing her dresser was on its side on the floor. Whatever had done that was strong. The dresser had to weigh almost a hundred pounds. What if she'd been in there? Or even Leah on the floor last night sleeping? She could have been killed.

"By the power of God the Father, the Son, and the Holy Spirit, I command whatever is in here to leave." Leah stepped inside and then glanced over at Mason. "Can you pick that thing up for us?" She turned quickly away. "And pull your robe together please."

He wrapped the robe tight and tied it closed with the belt before stepping over to lift the dresser from the floor, setting it upright.

It would have been kind of funny if Ashley wasn't so damned scared. This was the room that was under attack. Her hands shook as she poured the salt along the window and then the floor along the walls. She murmured the words along with Leah, adding a silent prayer that it would work.

Leah took her time, stepping slowly and blowing on the embers to increase the smoke. All the while she kept up the litany. Mason held the crystal high as he walked around the room. Finally they were done.

Ashley left a pile of salt in the middle of the floor on her rug and then along the door opening. She looked at Leah and bit her lower lip waiting.

"It's done. This room is cleansed. And I just know leaving the salt here will finish it. Demons and evil spirits hate salt."

"Kind of like garlic and vampires?" Mason's eyes smiled as he looked at her. For once he wasn't making fun though.

"Kind of."

But something wasn't right in Ashley's gut. This was too easy. "But this girl isn't evil, Leah. From the sounds of it, she was a victim. She wants her body to be found."

"And we'll do that once this bloody storm is over." Leah huffed a sigh and then proceeded to the stairs.

Ashley looked at Mason. "I'm still not sure about this."

"Well for now we have to trust that she knows what's she's doing. But your aunt has got to know about this. It's her house. You know that, right?"

"Yeah, I know it's her house."

"Now, who's being the smart-ass?" He smiled down at her.

When they got downstairs, Leah stood glaring at Maya. She turned to Ashley. "She tried to call your aunt. But the cell tower is out thank God." Her eyes narrowed looking at Maya. "You didn't have to do that you know! I fixed this!"

Preston jumped to Maya's defense. "Shu...she was scuh...scared, Leah! Besides, shu...she didn't get thru...through."

"Did it work? You really think it worked? No more crashes or faces in the window?" Henry kind of looked disappointed at that.

"Of course, it worked." Leah went over to the refrigerator and opened the door. "Anyone else want something to drink?"

"No thanks. I'm going to get changed though." Mason left the room heading for the laundry room.

The boys got up. Henry looked down at Maya. "No offense, Mayan, but pink looks better on you than me. C'mon Preston. Let's get out of these clothes."

When they left to join Mason, Ashley went over to Maya and sat down next to her. She handed the box of salt to her sister. "Here. You keep this with you. I'm not mad at you. We're telling Aunt Claire when she gets home. You're right about that."

A streak of lightning hitting the lake outside lit the room. Immediately a clap of thunder shook the house. Maya grasped Ashley's hand, almost jerking from her chair at the noise. But when the light in the kitchen zapped and extinguished, Ashley felt a shudder of dread flow through her shoulders.

What next?

TWENTY FOUR

Claire ended the call on her cell phone and slipped it into her purse. She looked across the desk as Ed Rowntree signed the last line of the offer to purchase the house on Maple. She was almost done here.

But her gut was tight with worry. She had called the girls four times since the storm had started and there was still no answer. From the "no service" message, it looked like the cell phone tower was out. But they weren't alone thank God. At least she hoped that Mason hadn't left them when the storm hit. But Leah would be there with the girls. She'd made sure of that.

Ed looked over at her. "So when will I know?" He rose from the chair and tossed the pen on the table.

Originally she had planned on presenting the offer to the owners right after she finished writing it up. "Tomorrow. I'll meet with them first thing tomorrow morning."

"Okay. I'll be waiting to hear from you." He smiled and left her office.

She was going home. She had no intention of hosting the open house for her boss. Ever since she'd left home, there'd been a growing knot of worry in her gut. There was something wrong. The girls had been up to something and she needed to talk to them ASAP. She knew herself well enough to know that it could be foolhardy if not dangerous to ignore that feeling.

Call it a sixth sense or whatever.

As she passed the secretary, she paused. "Something's come up at home. I can't do the open house. Gerry will be miffed but it is what it is."

Carol had been at the firm since Gerry had started it fifteen years ago. She looked up from her computer. "With this weather no one's going to be looking at houses. Besides, he'll be happy you made this sale today. Go home. Look after your kids."

"See you tomorrow." She opened the door as the older woman called out to "drive safe."

Even going the ten feet to her car had soaked through her blouse by the time she settled in behind the wheel. She started the car, driving slowly along streets that were rivers of rain. She turned on the radio before swiping her hand across the windshield clearing the condensation.

But after two minutes of some country artist crooning, she flipped the station off. She was way too tense to listen to that.

It seemed to take forever driving through the town and then out to the road where she lived. When she pulled into the driveway she breathed a sigh of relief seeing Mason's truck still parked there. At least they weren't alone. But her brow furrowed as she peered at the house. Not a light was on.

She hurried from the car and up the walkway to the house. She called out as she stepped inside, "Ashley? Maya? I'm home."

The kitchen was not only dark, it was empty. She strained to hear just as Ashley stepped into the kitchen. "Aunt Claire! Thank God you're here!"

Maya and Leah were right behind her. Maya rushed over and threw her arms around her waist. "Aunt Claire. We were so scared."

She hugged her niece and kissed the top of her head, noticing the guys file into the room as well. She looked down at Maya. "What's wrong, honey? It's just a storm."

Her gut was a tight knot watching the terror in the young girl's eyes. What the hell was going on?

Maya's eyes welled up with tears and she was about to speak but Ashley beat her to it.

"We did something really bad, Aunt Claire. We found a Ouija board in the attic and we tried to summon Mom and Dad. But something else came too."

"A Ouija board?" When they all nodded, she said, "Oh shit." Claire straightened and her breath hitched in her throat remembering her own experience when she was their age with a Ouija board. It had been a nightmare! She'd learned her lesson and threw it away to end the horror. Even so, haunted dreams plagued her for weeks. On top of that was a constant sense of seeing something just at the periphery of her vision. It was a terrible and eerie episode in her life. Her voice was icy when she spoke, "Where is it now?"

Ashley glanced at Leah and then she answered, "I don't know."

Claire put her arm around Maya's shoulders and walked her over to the table. "Sit down." She turned on Ashley and Leah. "What do you mean, you don't know? Did you throw it in the lake?"

Ashley took a deep breath and sat down next to Leah and Maya. "No. I put it in the trashcan. But when I went out to check it this morning it was gone."

Maya grabbed at Claire's arm and blurted, "I saw a face...a young woman in my window! And when we came back from looking for her body our rooms were trashed. The ghost was *here,* Aunt Claire. I saw her and she tore our rooms apart."

Leah jumped in trying to calm the situation. "I fixed it though, Claire. I used protection crystals, a sage smudge and salt. We cleansed the rooms. They're good now."

Claire's head was spinning from them rushing all the words at her. She slumped into the chair and stared at them. "Hang on. One at a time. Ashley, tell me what happened."

Ashley's eyes filled with tears. "We used it to contact Mom and Dad. I think we really reached them because they answered questions only they would know. But the second time, some other spirit took over. She spelled out her name.

Skylar. She told us that her body was in the circle—"

Maya interrupted, "The fairy circle!"

Claire turned to Maya and patted her arm. "Hush. Let Ashley continue." A fairy circle? Oh God.

Ashley looked at Maya and then back to Claire. "We found this clearing past that Kovac woman's house. Leah says it's a fairy circle and the ghost girl used that term too, so we'd know. She was murdered, Aunt Claire."

"And you didn't think this was important enough to *tell* me? You searched for a murdered girl's body?" Her back stiffened but she tried to appear calm. She was just barely able to. The only thing saving them was the fact they were terrified already.

"Yeah. You're right! I'm sorry we didn't! Anyway, the next day we found the Ouija board in my room even though we'd left it in Maya's. And later, Maya saw this girl's face in the window." Ashley glanced at Leah. "Leah did a cleansing ritual."

She turned back to Claire. "We were so scared that I put it into the trash, deep inside." Ashley was quiet for a few moments, looking at the table and then over at Maya. She spoke again, "Last night when I volunteered to go take the kitchen garbage out, the board was set up on the lid of the can. The reader was sitting on the word "No" like it was telling me I couldn't get rid of it."

Maya gasped before yelling in her face**,** "What? You never told me that!"

"Hush Maya!" Claire looked at Ashley. "And this morning it was gone? Is that it?"

"Yes." It came out as a small squeak. Ashley looked at her aunt and again her eyes welled. "We tried to find this Skylar's body today. The rain started so we had to come home."

"Don't forget the old gypsy I almost hit with the truck."

Claire sat back looking at Mason. It was the first time he'd spoken since she got home. Was he in on it too? "What about Mrs. Kovac?"

Ashley took a deep breath. "She was in the middle of the road, and Mason almost ran her over! She looked right at me and said "you" and then she turned to Leah and she said "you started this." When we got home we found our clothes..." Her voice hitched, but she plowed on. "Our clothes were thrown all over the bedroom floor!"

Henry held up his hand. "Wait! There's more!" He jerked a thumb at his older brother. "Mason saw her too! The face in the window!" Henry looked at his brother like he'd won the Indianapolis 500.

Preston stepped closer and put his hand on Maya's shoulder. "Thu...the duh...dresser crashed to the flu...floor right after."

"But we did the cleansing again. It really worked this time, Claire. Please don't tell my mom." Leah's lower lip pushed out doing her best puppy-dog look.

Claire sat back and said nothing, trying to digest all that they'd told her. From the corner of her eyes she could see them all staring at her, waiting for her to lower the boom. She needed a moment to think about this. And making them wait would serve them right. Anticipation of punishment was sometimes worse than the actual punishment.

She rose to her feet. "I'm going upstairs to change out of these damp clothes. When I come down we'll talk some more about this." Her usual smile was gone as she looked at each of them in turn. She walked out of the room and up the stairs, hearing silence behind her. Let them stew.

Opening the door to her room, she started unbuttoning her blouse. She wandered over to the bed and froze. All the air left the room as she saw what was on the bed.

The Ouija board.

And not just any Ouija board.

Her heart leapt in her chest seeing the scrawls in red ink across the lid. With growing dread she reached out and flipped the board over to see what she feared.

Her initials.

In red ink that she had scrawled there thirteen years ago.

TWENTY FIVE

"Your aunt is totally pissed." Henry looked at Maya and took a seat across the table from her. "I hope she doesn't ground you for the summer." He leaned over the table and grinned. "Shit, she's so pissed off, she'll probably ground me, and I don't even live here!"

Ashley sighed. "Shut up, Henry." She looked over to her sister. "I don't think it will last the summer, Maya. But maybe two weeks." There was a sense of relief, though. At least she wasn't lying or sneaking around anymore.

"I'll take the punishment. I just need to know that this is over." Maya's eyes narrowed when she looked at Ashley. "You should have told me the board was set up on the trashcan last night. And that it was missing this morning. I'm in this too, you know!"

Leah leaned to Maya. "She did it to protect you, silly." She looked up, blowing a gush of air through pursed lips, "Who's gonna protect me though? My mom is gonna ground me for life when she hears about this."

"Shhh. She's coming. I heard her bedroom door close." Mason walked over to stand behind Henry. He squeezed his brother's shoulders in his hands leaning over to whisper, "Try to be quiet for once will you? Don't make this worse than it is with your smart mouth."

They were deadly silent hearing the slow thud of Claire's feet on the stairs. With every step Ashley's neck muscles grew tighter and tighter. She looked over at the doorway when her aunt appeared.

Ashley's eyes flashed wide and her jaw dropped.

Oh. My. God. She had the Ouija board box in her hands, carrying it like it was a bomb.

"It was in your room?" Ashley sprung up from the seat.

Maya's voice was shrill, bordering on hysteria. "That can't be! I checked your room earlier, after our rooms were trashed. It wasn't there!"

Claire stopped a few feet from them. She looked down at the box containing the Ouija board and flipped it so that the bottom faced them. "Do you see those initials on the bottom?"

Preston who was the closest to her leaned over to look closely. "Cuh...C. V."

Aunt Claire looked dazed looking at each of them in turn. "Claire Vincent."

"That's a coincidence. It has to be." Mason muttered.

"I WROTE IT!" Claire's face was a knot of fear and the cords in her neck were taut and showing. "I was SEVENTEEN! I threw this board in a dumpster! HOW...How is this possible?"

Maya jumped up from her seat and ran to Ashley. She tried to comfort her sister, putting her arm around her waist and holding her close, while her own heart hammered fast. Maya openly cried, "I'm scared. Can we just go? Get out of here?"

Leah rose from her seat and took a step closer to Claire. "Maybe the Salter kids found it there. They could have brought it home? It was with their stuff in the attic."

Claire shook her head. "No. It found its way back to me. Somehow. Just like it kept moving from where you'd put it." She looked like she was barely holding herself together. Her hands shook and she almost stumbled walking across the room like a zombie.

Ashley stared at her. "What are you going to do, Aunt Claire?"

Her aunt's jaw was tight. "What I should have done back then. I'm going to burn this damn thing!"

Mason rushed over to her, "Hold on. It's raining, Claire. I'll put it outside. Whatever is left of it tomorrow, we'll destroy. I'll help you." He pried the board from her fingers and then turned to go to the door.

Ashley got up from her chair, about to go over to steady her aunt.

"SHIIIIIIT!"

The board flew up when Mason screamed. The lid flew off and Mason was a flurry racing across the room. "It's her! That face! She's at the door!"

Ashley jerked back grabbing Maya and staring with horror. Was she gonna come in?

Leah and Henry were the only ones to creep over to take a peek. Claire gripped the edge of the counter like she was holding a lifeline. Preston had moved to Maya's other side, putting his arm around her shoulder.

"Is she still there?" Mason's voice had raised a few octaves as he stood in the doorway next to the hall. "I swear. I saw her and she was *seriously* pissed off!"

"No. She's not there now." Leah stepped back looking down at the floor. "But you're not going to believe this."

Henry gasped when he looked down. "Holy Shit!" The board lay on the floor with the planchette centered over the word "No." He looked over at Maya. It was hard to tell if he was more scared or excited.

Claire pushed away from the counter and stepped over looking down at the board. "That does it! I'm destroying this damned thing!" She stomped on the reader and the pegs it rested on flew in three different directions. She bent to pick the board up.

CRASH! The whole house shook from the bang upstairs!

Claire froze while Mason screamed "Shit!" as he raced over

to join Ashley.

They stood in the semi darkness waiting while the wind and rain lashed the house outside.

Leah whispered loudly, "It's probably that dresser again."

The TV and the radio started blaring at full volume! Ashley jerked holding Maya even tighter.

"Thu...that's not possible. The power is off!" Preston shouted to be heard above the din. He looked over at Ashley and Mason.

Leah stepped over to him. "LET'S GET OUT OF HERE!"

The blaring stopped as quickly as it started, leaving Leah's words still ringing in the air.

Ashley grabbed her inhaler and took hit after hit of it deep into her lungs. Aunt Claire went over to her and rubbed her back; her eyes filled with tears. "Are you okay? Just breathe, Ash. We've got to get out of here. At least for today. We'll deal with all of this tomorrow."

Mason headed for the door and stopped dead in his tracks beside Henry. "We can't! She's still out there waiting for us!"

"Dude! She's gone." Henry looked disgusted for a moment and then he turned to Maya. "C'mon. This place is seriously screwed up."

Leah added. "No it's not. This can be fixed but not today. Not by me." She headed for the door and stopped when it refused to open. Pushing and twisting the handle, she gritted her teeth. "C'mon, you son of a bitch!" Her face was red from the effort when she turned. "The handle won't budge. We're locked in."

"No we're not!" Henry raced to the living room door leading out to the backyard. His grunts were followed by the sounds of his foot kicking at it. "Shit! It's locked too!"

Mason looked around the room and stopped when he looked out the window. "We'll break the window! It wants to keep us in here but it can't!" He grabbed a kitchen chair and lifted it stomping over to the big picture window.

Ashley looked at her aunt but it was like she'd given up. She didn't care that he'd be smashing her house. And the way things were going in there, who could blame her? She crossed her fingers and then turned as he hurled the chair at the glass.

But instead of the sounds of splintering, Mason yelped again.

She turned and saw him holding his arm and the chair was on the floor in pieces. His jaw dropped and he gaped at them. "It bounced off the glass! It should have gone through."

Claire straightened and her voice was flat when she spoke, "We're trapped. Whatever this thing is, it won't let us go."

Leah was crying as she held onto Preston's arm. She looked up at the ceiling, yelling, "WHAT DO YOU WANT? LET US GO. PLEASE!"

Preston's voice was low when he spoke, "We need to use the board again. She wants to tell us something."

Ashley stared at him feeling the hair on the back of her neck tingle. The thought of using the board made her blood run cold, but Preston had sounded so convincing. Again, his speech had been smooth like the other times he had used the board.

"Are you nuts? That's how this shit got started, Preston!" Mason glared at him and ran his fingers through his hair, making fists pulling it.

Aunt Claire nodded slowly. "He's right. We use it and this time we end it." She looked over at the board and yelled at it, "This is the last time!"

Leah picked the board up and looked at her brother, "How? She broke the reader. We won't know what it says."

Claire straightened and sneered at Leah before marching over to the cabinet. "Ever hear of a shot glass, little girl? I've got some experience with that damned board too." She plucked two small glasses out of the cabinet.

"Two? We don't need two." Leah cast a puzzled look at Claire and then set the board on the table.

"You're right." Claire reached into another cabinet and took a bottle of whisky down. As she poured she grimaced. "One for the board and one for me. It's been a long time. The last time I used this board, I saw my brother's death. It scared me so bad I threw it out. I thought if I did that, it wouldn't happen."

Ashley gaped at her aunt. "You saw Dad and Mom's death? Did you actually see it or—"

"That's not how that damned thing works Ash! You should know that. It spelled out the message." She poured the whisky and then lifted it to her lips, tossing it back in one swallow. There was a sad look in her eyes when she continued, "I thought Robert would be spared. I tried begging, pleading as I used that damned board. We know how well that worked out." She brought the other glass to the table and then took a seat.

She continued in a voice that was flat, "It possessed me. I had nightmares and would wake up to see a dark shadow hovering in the corner of my room. It got so bad that I saw it during the day, out of the corner of my eye and when I'd look, it would disappear. I had to get rid of it. But it wasn't through with me, apparently."

Ashley fought a fresh batch of tears as she took her seat, sliding her chair closer to Maya who was openly crying. She noticed that Leah looked down. At least this time she had enough sense not to pretend she knew what the hell she was doing, not in light of what Claire had just said.

Even Henry was quiet as he sat down next to Preston.

Mason looked around. "Where am I supposed to sit?"

Preston looked up at him. "Guess you'll have to stand. You broke your chair."

Ashley smiled and looked around to see that Preston's remark had eased some of the tension.

Mason muttered, "Very funny." He squeezed in next to Ashley, bending and extending his hand toward the shot glass in the center of the board.

"Just your index finger of your left hand." Aunt Claire placed hers there first.

"Shouldn't we have a candle?" Leah's eyes were narrow peering at Claire.

Aunt Claire shot a look at Leah which was enough to snap

her mouth shut and join everyone with a fingertip on the glass. Claire gazed at the small object for a few moments silently before she spoke, "We approach, in peace, whatever spirit resides here. I know that you are here. Are you the spirit of the girl who appeared earlier?"

Ashley glanced over at her aunt. Whatever shock she'd suffered when she first saw the board was not in the confident way she spoke then. She was more like the aunt she'd always been. Maya sniffled next to her and her hand rose to swipe a tear threatening to drip from her jaw. Even a look at Henry showed him waiting expectantly for something to happen. Like her, he was a believer now.

It was deathly still, except for the sounds of their breathing and the white noise of the rain continuing outside. The glass edged slowly across the board and then picked up speed to stop directly over the word "Yes."

Claire took a deep breath staring down at the "reader," "Skylar, what is it you wish of us?"

The reader moved faster now, shooting to the letters, "F," "I," "N," "D," "B," "O," "D" and then to the letter "Y." "Find body." Aunt Claire was about to ask another question but the reader kept moving. "F," "I," "N," "D," "K," "I," "L," "L," "E" and then "R." Claire's forehead creased. "Find killer."

Henry whispered, "Why can't she just tell us who killed her?"

Ashley looked at her aunt. It was something she was wondering too.

Leah hissed over at Henry, "She's probably not allowed, jerk."

"He's not a jerk. Cut that out, Leah." Mason glared at her. "It makes sense to me too."

Aunt Claire shot each of them a look. "Shush." She turned back to the reader. "You've told us where your body can be found. We promise we'll do everything we can to find your remains. Please spell out the name of the person who caused your death."

The reader began doing wide circles around the board.

Ashley held her breath saying a silent prayer it wouldn't fly off the board before they could properly end the session with "Goodbye." Although from all the scary things happening in the house, her spirit was already there creating havoc.

"Stop this! You're angry. We get that. But you need to settle down and tell us. Spell it out or we stop." Claire used her "no nonsense" voice, and her eyes were narrow.

The reader paused and then shot to the letter "T," "O" and jerked back to the letter "O." But it wasn't finished. It went to "L," "A," "T" and then "E."

"Too late?" Leah looked over at Claire. "What does that mean?"

BANG! BANG! BANG!

Ashley just about jumped out of her skin! It came from the kitchen door! Maya's finger left the board and she clambered over onto Ashley's lap.

BANG! BANG! BANG! "LEAH!"

Leah screamed, "It's come for me!" She jumped up and ran out of the room.

Preston stood up and crept over to the door slowly. "It's a man out there! There's someone at the door!"

Claire shoved the shot glass across the board to the word "Goodbye." She looked at Ashley. "That's how you end a session." She got to her feet and took a deep breath. "Someone's at the door. That's all. It's just someone knocking on the damned door!"

Ashley looked at her aunt and wondered if she was trying to convince them or herself that it wasn't related.

"You can't open it, remember? And it might be the killer!" Mason followed her, walking slowly. He grabbed the bottle of whisky holding it like a club.

Claire grasped the door handle and peeked out the window before she turned it. "What the..." Her hand moved quickly and the handle turned easily. Mason was right behind her with the bottle ready to clobber whomever entered.

She yanked the door open and cried out, "Jake?"

"Claire?"

Ashley sprung to her feet tugging Maya after her. It was unreal! Her uncle Jake!

Jake held a gun high and smiled up at Mason. "My gun beats that bottle kid but I'll take a drink if you don't mind." He looked back at Claire. "Where's Leah? Who is Leah? Can I come in out of the rain at least?"

When he stepped inside Ashley raced toward him and threw her arms around his neck. "Uncle Jake!" Tears once more rolled down her cheeks but this time it was relief and happiness at seeing him.

"Ashley! And Maya! Oh my God! What are you doing here? Shouldn't you be home with your mom and dad?" He hugged them one handed, holding the gun high out of reach. "Not that it's not great to see you but..." He pulled back and looked at them.

Ashley was openly bawling now, heart-wracking sobs and it was Maya who answered, "They're...they're dead, Uncle Jake." She took a step back while Claire hurried forward to tuck her into her arms.

Claire spoke next, "They were killed in a car accident two years ago, Jake."

"What? Oh my God." He pulled Ashley into him again, kissing the top of her head. "You poor, poor kids. I'm so sorry. I didn't know. Oh God."

Leah broke the moment when she spoke, "Angela? She sent you, didn't she?"

"Are you Leah?"

She nodded. "Angela said you helped her family with a ghost in Alexandria Bay."

He nodded.

"She said you're in the FBI?"

"Yeah." He reached into his back pocket and pulled out a leather wallet, flipping it open to display his badge and ID card. "FBI" was printed in large letters next to his picture.

"Holy shit!" Henry said. "Like the *X-files*? There's a real X-files and you work for them?"

"No," Jake said, putting his ID back in his pocket. "Angela

and her family…" he hesitated. "They were under our protection because of a case. That's all I can say."

Leah nodded. "Yeah, she wouldn't say anything about that either. But she said that you'd believe her."

"I did, that's why I came right away." He reached out and held Ashley close as he stepped farther into the room. "She said you were in trouble. Something to do with a murder and..." He hesitated a moment. "...ghosts."

He looked over at the table and then at each of them before fixing an icy stare at Claire. "What's going on here, Claire? And why the hell didn't you let me know about Rob and Gail? They were my friends as well as my sister and brother-in-law."

The door slammed shut behind him with a force that shook the house. He jerked and then spun around with his gun in hand. But before he could even come to a standstill, a crash upstairs reverberated through Ashley's gut.

She looked over at her aunt and her voice was a soft whisper, "It's happening again."

TWENTY SIX

"What the hell was that?" Jake raced over to the doorway and then looked up the stairs,

The pounding continued. It was like every door in the upstairs slammed shut and then opened again to slam again.

"It's her! She wants us to find her body! She's not going to leave us alone until we do!" Ashley screamed to be heard above the banging.

Jake spun around scowling at Claire. "Salt! Where's your damned salt!" He raced to the cabinets and flung the doors wide, shoving things aside to find it.

Claire raced over and opened a bottom door. She grabbed the box and handed it to him. "Here! But it isn't going to work! We need to find her body! That's what she wants!"

He looked at her. "We need to settle this thing down! Can't you see these kids are scared out of their minds!" He looked over at Ashley and Maya. "Screw that! We need to get out of this place. Now!"

Henry raced for the door, just ahead of Mason. He pulled and yanked at the door. "She's locked us in again! We're trapped here!"

"What do you mean? I just came *in* that door!" Jake banged the salt down and with a few wide strides he was there, elbowing by the guys. He pushed and pulled trying to get the handle to move. Finally he turned away. "Damn it!"

Mason huffed a fast sigh. "Even the windows won't break for us to get out. I tried it already."

Preston shouted, "No! We haven't finished doing the board! We need to go back and finish it!"

"He's right! There's more she wants to tell us!" Leah raced over to the table and took a seat.

Ashley stood still silently crying as she watched her friend set the shot glass back in the center of the board. God. Just make this stop. She trudged lifting her hands to cover her ears from the bedlam in the floor above them.

Maya sat next to her while Preston sat on her other side.

"Claire? What the hell are you doing fooling around with Ouija boards? You shouldn't have this thing and more importantly, not use it with kids. For God's sake, Claire!"

But Ashley tuned her uncle out, raising her hand to join the others. Even Henry and Mason had come over to the table. They all placed their fingertips on the shot glass as before.

Leah began, "Skylar. We need—"

"No! I'll do it this time!" Preston wasn't taking no for an answer.

"Your voice, Preston. What's with—"

"Be quiet Henry! Let him do it!" Maya gave his leg a kick under the table.

Preston started again, "Skylar. We need to—"

"Skylar! Wait a minute! I *know* that name! There's a missing person alert that just came out."

Ashley looked over at her uncle. "Uncle Jake! Please we need to do this." Of course they knew she was missing. She was dead.

"Can I just do this please?" Preston shot a look over at Claire and Jake before turning to the board. "Skylar who killed you? We want to help."

Once more the reader refused to cooperate at first going in small circles. From the corner of her eyes Ashley saw her uncle go out to the hallway and start up the stairs.

The reader jerked over to the letter "L." It started up again but before it could stop at the next letter, Claire's scream pierced through the kitchen.

Ashley jerked back and looked over at her aunt! Claire's eyes nearly popped out on her cheeks, staring at the door.

"I saw her! She looked straight at me! Oh my God!" One hand clutched the edge of the counter while her other hand rose to cover her throat.

Jake flew back into the kitchen. "What happened?" He rushed over to Claire. "Are you all right?"

She turned and fell into his arms. "No! It was her! That Skylar girl!"

The board was forgotten in the rush over to look out the window.

Mason looked at Claire. "The face. It was just black holes where her eyes should have been, right? And she looked really angry, right?"

Claire nodded. She looked up at Jake and stepped back from him. "I can't take much more of this. None of us can take any more!"

Preston went back to the board and yelled, glaring down at it, "Stop this!" He touched the glass reader. "We want to help you! Can't you *get* that!"

Ashley went over, watching him. When Leah stepped to the other side of the table she looked at Preston and then turned to Ashley. "Let him do this alone. There's something..." Her voice trailed off as she watched the reader jerk across the board, pausing for a fraction of a second at the letters, answering him.

L I A R It spelled the word liar. It was about to repeat when Preston yelled.

"I don't speak so good but I don't lie! I'll prove it! I won't spit swear, I'll blood swear! Blood for blood!" Preston picked up the glass and smashed it on the edge of the table. He sliced his finger with a shard, watching his hand as blood immediately ran from the cut.

He slammed his hand on the board spattering blood over it. "There! Now stop this! We will find your body first thing in the morning when the rain stops. I swear a blood oath to you, Skylar!"

Suddenly all was silent. Only the hiss of the rain outside disturbed the air. And the air—it seemed lighter and easier to breathe for Ashley. She looked at Preston. "You did it."

Maya went over and lifted his hand from the board. "You did it. You also really did a number on your finger, Preston." More blood oozed out and dripped onto the board.

"I duh...don't know whu...what came over muh...me." He smiled down at her. "It wuh...worked though."

"Yeah…yeah it did." She swiped a tear from her eyes with her other hand, not letting go of his injured one.

In the background Ashley heard Jake whisper to Claire, "What's with his speech?"

The lights came on, and the buzz of the refrigerator starting up made Ashley look around. It was only in the glare of the light that she realized how dark it had been in the kitchen.

"Let there be light." Henry came over and clapped Preston on the back. "You did it, bud!"

Mason dashed over to try the door. It opened as easily as it ever had. "Hey! We're not trapped anymore. We can actually go home now, Henry!"

Preston turned and shouted, "No! We all stay here tonight. I gave my word. We fix this! We don't call the police or anyone else. We're in this together!"

Ashley looked at him. Preston was adamant about all this and considering he'd managed to restore some kind of order in the house, they had to listen to him.

"Well, technically, the cops already kind of know, right?" Jake said pointing at himself.

Claire had grabbed bandages and paper towels and was administering to Preston's cut. She looked over at Jake. "You could have knocked me over with a feather seeing you at the door."

Leah took her phone out of her pocket to try it. "They must have fixed the cell tower. I'll let Mom know you're staying the night, Preston." She stepped across the kitchen, and her voice was a low murmur from the living room when she spoke on the phone.

Ashley was still in shock waiting and watching for the lights to go out or the upstairs to start banging again. But Preston looked confident, even smiling as Claire applied the bandage. He had some kind of connection to the board and the girl. The smoothness of his words was evidence of that.

"I'll take that soft drink now if the offer's still open."

Claire looked at Henry, answering him, "Help yourself. They're in the fridge. I think they should still be cold."

She finished with the bandage and then went over to the counter, pouring another whisky for herself. "After all that I need this." She looked at Jake. "How 'bout you? You always liked scotch."

Ashley watched her uncle's face grow tight, watching Aunt Claire with flinty eyes. He practically spat his next words, "There are a lot of things I'd like right now. Yeah, scotch is one but more importantly I want some answers, Claire."

Mason shot a look at Claire and Jake and then sidled close to Ashley talking out of the side of his mouth, "From the look on his face, your aunt is in serious shit. Just when we thought things had calmed down."

TWENTY SEVEN

How could you keep your brother's death from me, Claire?" Jake grabbed the glass from her hand and glared at her.

Her heart skipped a beat as her mind scrambled. She looked over at her nieces and their friends. They'd just been through a horrifying time. *She* was barely holding it together. How were *they* managing?

She looked at Jake, saw the anger and sadness in his eyes and her chest sank. "Look, I was not doing well at the time. Surely, you can understand that. And do we really want to get into all that now? Here, in front of the kids?"

"Why not? It concerns them too! You shut me out of their lives. You kept your brother's death from me! Claire! Rob and I were buddies! I loved him and Gail like they were my own brother and sister! You couldn't pick up the phone and let me know?"

Claire gazed at Ashley and Maya. They were standing with tears in their eyes reliving that time. How could Jake be so insensitive? She couldn't change the past! And besides...

"You walked out on me, Jake! I was hurt and angry! I

couldn't stand the thought of seeing you again!"

There! It was the truth. She'd been a mess, hiding out at her big brother's home to try—somehow try!—to get over it. She took a fast swallow of the whisky and slammed the glass on the counter. Barely able to stop the tears that stung the back of her eyes, she took a deep breath.

His voice was ominous in the softness of his tone, "Who's fault was that, Claire?"

She looked over at her nieces and then turned on him, "Don't go there, Jake. Not here in front of the girls." She opened the fridge and got the plate of burgers out trying to focus on the mundane task of cooking and getting them something to eat. She was not going to get sucked into this argument.

Jake's hand gripped her wrist. "Why not? They're my nieces too! For someone who never wanted kids, you're in the thick of it now, aren't you! I could have been part of Ashley and Maya's lives. Could have helped them through the ordeal. You've deprived not only me, but you hurt them as well, Claire!"

He tossed back the glass of whisky in one quick move. Turning to her again, he sneered. "How's that career working out for you, Claire? Are you top sales agent in Saranac Lake? Is it everything you've dreamed of?"

It was a battle not to reach up and slap him! How dare he say all those things in front of the girls! And if he loved them so much...

"You could have called them! Why didn't you? Huh, Jake? Answer that!"

BANG!

Claire jerked and she looked at the ceiling overhead. It was happening again! Oh God, no!

"Yu...you need to stop fighting." Preston's face had flared, and he looked down after saying the words. "I think if you keep yelling at each other, it reminds her of her own death. Can you just stop?"

Henry's eyes held panic and mirth as he pointed to the

ceiling. "Yeah! Don't make momma ghost come down here!"

Mason snorted. "You're such a tool, man."

Claire looked over at Jake through a film of tears. She couldn't put the kids or herself through anymore terror. Jake was hurting and he had a right to that hurt. But Preston was right. Fighting was making things worse.

Jake set the glass on the counter. "I'm going upstairs to see if anything's broken up there. If you don't mind, Claire, I want to spend some time alone with my nieces." He turned to Ashley and Maya. "Girls. Can you come up, and we can talk while we check it out?"

They nodded and followed him out of the kitchen silently.

Claire stood crying as she stood at the counter. This was all too much. The nightmare of the Ouija board, her house possessed by an angry spirit and seeing that face. For a moment she paused staring down at the floor. That face.

"Do you need help with this, Claire?" Leah stood looking up at her. "I'm sorry, I had no idea Angela knew Jake. I mean, I'm glad he's here but he really lit into you."

Claire's mind snapped back to Jake. Again the tears flowed. She'd really blown it with him. She'd made a mistake that couldn't be fixed

TWENTY EIGHT

Ashley looked over at maya as they followed their uncle up the stairs. He wasn't angry with them but he'd sure torn a strip off their aunt. It had been scary how mad both of them had been. Not as scary as the Ouija board crap or the Skylar thing, but scary nonetheless.

"I want you to know that I love you. I'm really sorry about what happened to your parents." Jake paused and looked back at them, searching their faces. "I loved your dad and mom."

Ashley nodded. She could see the earnest look in his eyes, that he meant every word.

"Why didn't you ever call us?" Maya blurted.

"Honey, if I'd known what you were going through, wild horses could not have kept me away." He looked down at the step where Ashley's foot rested. "I never heard from her, nor her brother… I figured they just took her side and wrote me out of their lives." He raised his head. "I never knew they died."

He sighed again. "I called your dad about a two months after your aunt and I broke up, you know. I had moved to Syracuse. The phone was no longer in service."

Ashley said, "They died a week after you two broke up, Uncle Jake. Maya and I were living with Aunt Claire by then." The bottom of her chin trembled. "We thought you didn't care…" She shot a look of fury down the stairs. "She screwed up."

Nodding, Jake said, "I know." He looked back at Maya, "But even through that I still loved you. I missed you too. But I was wrong to never call, or try harder to reach out to you guys. I know that now. Please, will you forgive me?"

Ashley took a deep breath. "We never reached out to you either, Uncle Jake."

"Honey, you lost your parents. No, this is my bad."

"Okay, then. Of course I forgive you, Uncle Jake. But we need to see you, talk to you more."

Maya looked over at Ashley and then turned to Jake. "I'll forgive you if you make this right. Ash has a point. You need to make time for us in your life. Visit us."

Jake reached for both of them and drew them into a group hug. "I will. I promise." He held them for a few moments and then eased away. "Now, we've got some catching up to do. Let's see what mess is up there and you can tell me while we get it cleaned up."

He turned and then flicked the light switch on at the top of the stairs. All the doors were open in every room, but there was nothing out of the ordinary in the hallway.

As he walked into the bathroom, Maya began, "Aunt Claire's got a boyfriend. Neither one of us like Puke Ass."

He stopped dead, taken aback. He lowered his head. "Really? Who? She's got a boyfriend?"

Ashley shot a look at Maya and then added, "His name is Lucas Moretti."

Jake nodded and looked around the bathroom. He turned and came back out, speaking casually, "Oh yeah? How long she been seeing him?"

Ashley hid the smile following him to Maya's room. He was pretty interested in what was going on with her aunt for a guy that was through with her. "A few months…maybe about a year or so. Are you seeing anyone?"

He stopped and bent to pick up the dresser which had toppled over, setting it straight before he answered, "No. I'm too busy with work. Just some dates here and there, no one special." He looked around the room and then up at the attic hatch. "Let me guess. That's where you found the board, right?"

Maya gaped at him. "How'd you know?"

"Just a hunch." He looked at Ashley. "How about you? You interested in that Mason guy? He sure seems interested in you."

Ashley could feel her face getting warm. "Maybe." She left the room and then went down to her own bedroom. Again the dresser was overturned and even the bed was moved, now up against the window. Holy cow! This ghost was pretty strong!

Jake straightened the bed and then set the dresser upright. "How's school? Doing well there, you two?"

Maya scoffed. "It's summer, Uncle Jake."

He reached out and pinched her side, trying to tickle her. "I know that, Miss Smarty-Pants! Did you pass or what?"

Ashley walked past him and grinned. "Straight A's except in math and science."

"Hey! I could give you a hand with that." He followed her down the hall and then to the other side to their aunt's bedroom.

"How? Don't you live in Syracuse? That's a pretty far way to go to help us with our homework." Maya moaned as she followed him into the room.

"This room wasn't touched." Ashley turned to her uncle. "It was only where we used the board. I wish I'd burned it like I'd planned." Her face was tight when she continued, "Yet, it's the same board that Aunt Claire used as a teenager. How weird is that? It turned up in here on her bed."

"She said the board told her that Dad would die. She threw it away and yet it was here in this house that she bought." Maya looked up at him. "It sort of followed her. Do you think we will ever be free of it?"

He looked at each of them. “Yes. When this is all over I’ll make sure of it. I’m not leaving till I know you girls are safe.”

Maya went over to him and hugged him. “I don’t want you to go. Can you get a transfer at work and live here?”

He stroked her hair and looked down at her. “I promise I’ll come see you. And I’ll call you.” He looked over at Ashley. “We can Skype so I can help you with math.”

Ashley stepped forward and went up on her toes to kiss his cheek. “I’d like that, Uncle Jake.”

Maya pulled back and looked up, “Who is this Angela who knows you and Leah?”

He chuckled. “That’s story in itself, Maya. And not one I’d care to get into right now. Let’s just say she’s a kid who has seen more than enough of life and the afterlife.”

“I’ve got to hear it!” Maya gave him a squeeze and tried to tickle his waist.

Ashley smiled and went out of the room to go back downstairs. “Not me! If it has to do with demons and angry spirits, I’m good.”

Maya continued behind her with Jake. “You can sleep in my room. I’ll bunk with Ash and Leah.”

He laughed. “Sounds like a plan. I’ve had more than enough of couch surfing.” When Ashley turned to peer at him, he added, “I have a place. But I’ve had to bunk on sofas guarding people, for work.”

She smiled and continued down the stairs.

TWENTY NINE

The smell of the burgers broiling in the oven drifted to Ashley's nostrils. It was only then that she realized she hadn't eaten since that morning. When she walked into the kitchen, Mason and Leah were at the counter helping with the dinner. Henry and Preston were seated at the kitchen table, but the Ouija board was gone.

"What'd you do with it, Preston?" Maya went over and took a seat next to him.

Henry answered, "We took it out to the garden shed. But who knows if it's gonna stay there?"

Ashley's gut wrenched at his words because he was right. The board had a mind of its own and a way of appearing wherever it chose. When this was over, she was not only going to burn it but she would bury the ashes...on the other side of town.

A cell phone started up and after a few notes Ashley recognized the tune as the one her aunt had selected for Lucas's calls. Aunt Claire dried her hands and raced over to her purse. She looked at the front of her phone and then looking around. "I've got to take this." She hurried out of the room and answered it.

Maya looked over at Ashley, "Great. He calls *after* the shit storm is over. He's a big help."

All the while Jake was quiet watching them. Ashley nodded

and then spoke to Leah, "Your mom was okay with Preston staying? She didn't think that was kind of weird?"

Leah shrugged, "She was probably more relieved that we wouldn't be out driving around in this storm. She said that the street in front of the house is flooded. She's got Dad going downstairs every fifteen minutes making sure the sewers aren't backing up into the basement."

Mason turned from where he was cutting vegetables and looked at Jake. "You said something earlier about Skylar. That you saw a missing person alert come through. It has to be the same one, right? I mean that name is not too common."

"Yeah." Jake looked at Ashley as he took his cell phone from his pocket. "I want to go online; is your internet up?"

"I think so…I mean, it was earlier today, but who knows…" She looked to the ceiling. "If Skylar's messed it up?"

Jake's eyebrows rose. "Well, let's find out." He tapped his screen. "Yep, you got Wi-Fi." He typed on the small keyboard and brushed the screen with the tips of his finger, scanning through pages. He paused and then walked over to Mason. "You said you saw her in the window. Is this her?"

Mason pulled back and his eyes went wide. "Yeah. That's the face I saw earlier."

Maya jumped from her seat ahead of the boys racing over to see the photo. "Yeah. That's her. Who was she? Are you going to let them know that she's dead?"

Jake looked at Preston. "I think you're right that it needs to be just us. We'll look for her tomorrow morning. Plus, what would I tell them if I called it in? I know she's dead because you guys saw her ghost? It's better to wait until I have hard evidence." He sighed. "Like her body."

Ashley turned away and took some things out of the fridge. She could barely look at that poor girl's face knowing she was dead. And not just dead but desperately reaching out for their help. The girl didn't look that much older than she was herself.

"Did she live around here? When was she last seen?" Henry stared at Jake.

Jake held the phone back and read, "Nineteen years old,

last seen at the Akwesasne casino." He looked at Henry. "That's about an hour away."

Maya piped up, "Carol works there! I wonder if she saw her."

"Who's Carol?" Jake asked.

Ashley set the ketchup and mayo on the counter. "She's a friend of Aunt Claire's. She's an accountant at the casino." She looked over at the doorway and heard Claire's voice from the living room. She must be telling Puke Ass all about what was going on.

Jake put his phone back in his pocket and then went over to check the burgers in the oven. "Just in time. I guess your aunt forgot about them." His voice was barely audible in the next words, "Too busy with her boyfriend."

Leah finished with the salad and brought it over to the table. "So... Angela? How do you know her, Jake? She's on the West Coast."

Jake took the tray out and scowled. "She shouldn't be broadcasting that fact on social media, Leah. I knew her and her family briefly in Alexandria Bay."

Leah stood watching him put the burgers in buns and place them on the plates that Ashley passed him. "She's in my Facebook group. I told her what was happening here with the Ouija board and that spirit. She said she knew someone who has some experience with that who wasn't that far away from here. So tell us. What happened?"

Maya joined in, "Yeah, you said something about the afterlife. I want to hear about it."

Ashley was about to object but Preston beat her to it. "I...I don't thu...think thu...that's such a good i...idea right now. Thu...things are quiet. Luh...let's just go wih...with that."

Ashley took the cutlery from the drawer and handed the bundle to Mason to set the table. "Preston is right. We've been through enough. Maybe some other time we can hear that story."

Jake's face had tightened. "Don't hold your breath, Ash." He looked over at the doorway. "Is she going to be on the phone all night? How often does she see this clown? What's he do for a living anyway?"

Ashley rolled her eyes. "He's a hedge fund investment guy. He works from home."

Henry sneered. "No, that's what he says he does. If he's in the market then I'm a monkey's uncle."

Maya piped up, "Henry is obsessed with Wall Street. He's going to be a trader when he gets older."

Mason nudged his brother's shoulder as he passed him. "He'll make a ton of money to finance my dream of being a ski bum." He looked at Maya. "Where are we sleeping tonight by the way? Maybe we can take your room and you can bunk with your aunt or Ashley?"

Jake's finger rose in the air wagging it at Mason. "No, no, no. That's not how this works. I get Maya's room and you guys battle it out for the sofa. And remember, Mason. I'm a light sleeper and Ashley's uncle." He smiled brightly. "I also have a gun."

Ashley felt her face heat up, and she sneaked a glance at Mason. But instead of protesting that they were just friends and he already had a girlfriend, he chuckled looking at her uncle.

"You're all right, Jake!"

Jake shot a look at him. "Considering the situation how we're all in this together, I'll let you away with that. Normally it would be Mister Whitaker."

Aunt Claire came into the room at that moment and looked around. "Sorry. I see you got dinner yourselves. What are you talking about?"

Jake picked up his plate and cutlery and wandered over to the doorway. "I'm going to eat in the living room and check out your cable channels."

Ashley looked at her aunt and saw her cheeks flare red as she strode over to the table.

And just like that, the mood changed with everyone quietly eating.

THIRTY

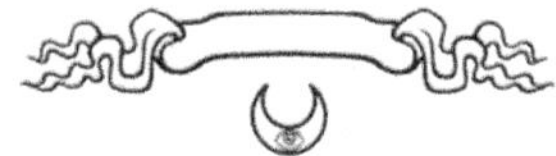

The sun was barely up the next morning when there was a tap at Ashley's bedroom door. "Ashley? Maya? Time to get up."

She blinked hard not recognizing the voice. Her brain shook the slumber remembering that Jake was there now. She rubbed Maya's shoulder. "C'mon. We've got to get up." She looked down at the floor where Leah was curled in a ball with just the top of her head showing in the folds of the sleeping bag.

"Leah. Wake up." Ashley threw the comforter back and Maya immediately grabbed for it.

"Just five more minutes."

She looked out the window and saw the rays of the sun reflecting orange streaks across the lake. Birds chirped outside, and she heard the small thuds of her uncle walking down the stairs.

She got up and pulled her robe over her shoulders. "C'mon you guys! Let's get this over with. You can take a nap this afternoon." She stepped past Leah who was rubbing her eyes as she sat up.

Thankfully there was no one in the bathroom and she could at least brush her teeth before facing the day. With any luck it would be Jake who found the body. At least he had experience in death and corpses. *If* they found the body that is.

When she finished in the bathroom and went back to her room to get changed, Maya and Leah were just coming out, dressed in jeans and sweatshirts. Maya muttered as she went past, "This couldn't wait till eight? This is waaaay too early to get up."

"Quit complaining." She went into her room and changed into long pants and a cotton shirt with long sleeves. Everything was bound to be sodden with rainwater in the fairy circle, and she remembered the scratches from the underbrush.

When she got downstairs, her uncle had taken control of the situation standing at the counter like a sergeant major handing each of them a glass of orange juice.

Maya looked over at her. "No breakfast. Just juice, in case what we find is gruesome. You know."

Claire wandered in and looked over at Jake. "I'll take the girls with me, and the guys can go with you."

He shook his head. "No. The girls are coming with me." He glanced over at Mason. "You should bring your truck as well. But remember, if we find her, we don't disturb the scene. I'll call the police and they can do their investigation."

"Wuh...we'll find her. I know it." Preston was the first one out the door.

Henry was at his heels. "I'm going to check the shed to see if that board is where we left it."

A few minutes later having downed her juice, Ashley stepped outside. Henry was just coming out of the shed and he looked disappointed. "It's still there."

Her eyebrows bobbed higher, looking over at Maya. "Good. Maybe this will be the end of it."

Maya nodded and followed her uncle down the driveway where his SUV was parked. Ashley wondered if it was his or if it was a department issue. It looked pretty new.

She sighed, mentally berating herself for being so shallow.

They were on the way to find a girl's body. A girl who had been callously murdered and she was thinking of her uncle's ride? That was sick.

Leah fell into step beside her and looked over, "We probably would have found her yesterday if not for the storm. I hope an animal hasn't gotten to her body."

The orange juice she'd drank earlier rose to the back of Ashley's throat as a picture of the mangled girl flashed in her brain. Eeew.

Her uncle opened his door and got inside. "You tell me where to stop since you've been there."

When Ashley was settled in the seat next to him, Maya chimed in, fully awake and raring to go now. "There's the old lady's house after we go around the bend in the road and then it's not far after that. I wonder if she'll run out at us like she did before."

"Not likely at this hour of the day." Ashley snapped her seat belt on and looked over at her uncle. "If we do find Skylar's body, you might want to question the old lady. She might have seen something."

"Don't worry, she'll be the first person the police will question if we turn up anything." He turned and backed out of the driveway onto the road.

Ashley saw her aunt's car and then Mason's truck behind them. She watched the road on each side, dreading the task ahead. After the night they'd spent, plus having her aunt and uncle with them made this trip all the more real. And Preston with that weird sense he'd developed, had been pretty sure.

As they came to the old lady's cottage, Ashley's jaw fell open. The old crone's car was parked there but the front door was wide open. She peered at the door half expecting the old witch to come flying out.

Leah must have been watching the house too because she commented, "That's weird. I wonder what she's doing leaving her door wide open like that."

Jake slowed down and then wheeled the suburban into the old lady's driveway.

Ashley looked over at him. "What are you doing?"

He put the car in park and looked over at her. "Call it a cop's Spidey sense, but I've learned to never ignore it. It's a strong suspicion that's usually right. I just want to check this out and talk to the old gal before we get there."

When he got out of the vehicle, Ashley stared at him walking over to the small stoop and then tap on the door. He looked back briefly and then disappeared inside.

Maya piped up from behind her. "Aunt Claire and Mason are parked on the side of the road, behind us. I honestly don't know what Uncle Jake hopes to achieve here. We should just get going and start looking in the fairy circle."

"Yeah. Preston said she was there. And he seems to be tuned in with this spirit." Leah added.

Ashley continued to watch the empty door opening. She glanced to the side of the house when movement flashed there. She stared hard but there was nothing but an old wooden shed beside some high bushes. But she could have sworn she saw a flash of red and a young woman for a moment.

Waitaminnit. Red?

Jake came out and hurried over to the vehicle. When he got in he started the car and turning to back out of the driveway, his words were clipped, "No old lady, but I think I saw a young girl in a red hoodie at the edge of the yard."

"I saw her too! She was running past that shed and then I lost sight of her in the bush."

Leah leaned forward, her hand on the back of Ashley's seat. "What's a young woman doing out at this time of day? It's barely light out."

Ashley turned across the backseat. "Leah? Your new blouse you wore yesterday; what color is it?"

"Emerald green. You saw me in it."

Ashley felt the color drain from her face. "When we were in the woods yesterday, I saw someone wearing something red through the trees. I thought it was you…"

"Wasn't me." Leah's eyes bulged. "Oh man…" She pointed back to the old woman's house and then up toward where they were heading. "You think it could be…?" They stared at each other quietly.

"What about the old witch? Maybe she turned herself into someone young?"

Uncle Jake glanced at Maya. "Now that's just crazy. But it is odd that the old lady wasn't there and this girl was."

When they got back on the road and had gone a little way, Ashley pointed to the area where the path began. Another flash of red and a girl's long, blond hair had been there for a micro-second. "Did you see her? She's going down the path!"

Jake pulled the car over to the side of the road and turned it off. "Yeah? How'd she manage to get down here so fast?"

Maya's hand was on the door handle. "See? Maybe that witch did something! She's some kind of shape-shifter or something."

"That's crazy." Ashley got out of the car and followed her uncle over to the break in the fence.

Aunt Claire stepped over and looked up at Jake. "Did you talk to Mrs. Kovac, the old lady?"

Jake shook his head. "No, I checked the house but she wasn't around. There was a young woman in a red hoodie—"

"I saw her too!" Preston started down the path. "C'mon!"

Ashley walked quickly beside her aunt going down the path, trying to avoid the wet branches and underbrush that were still wet from the day before. She looked over at Claire. "Did you see her?"

Claire shook her head. "No. I wonder why she'd be at Mrs. Kovac's house? And now here?"

Henry brushed by them running ahead to catch up with Preston. "Little red riding hoodie! I want to see what her game is."

Ashley rolled her eyes. Trust Henry to make light of looking for a dead girl. He skipped by Maya and Leah, almost tripping over a tree root in the process.

"Don't go in the fairy circle, Henry. Stay on the perimeter!" Leah called after him.

Mason was behind her, his feet squishing in the soft packed

earth of the trail. "I have to be at work for ten. I hope we find this Skylar soon. If not, I'm gonna have to leave you here."

Aunt Claire turned and shot a dirty look at him. "I think your boss will understand if we find a dead girl's body and you're late."

"Yeah. Shit. Sorry. That was kind of cold, wasn't it?"

Ashley shook her head. "Ya think?"

Jake and the rest of the troupe halted just up ahead and in a few moments Ashley and her aunt stood with them waiting for directions.

Jake's voice was low, "Leah said this fairy circle's about twenty feet in that direction. When we get there, we branch out." He pulled the collar of his jacket higher and turned following Leah.

Whether it was the chill of the early morning or the task ahead, Ashley shivered making her way through the wet trees. Every now and then a large, icy drop of rain fell from a high branch onto her head, while her sneakers were completely drenched from the underbrush.

"Hold it right there!" a harsh voice shouted.

She looked up and saw her uncle, Preston, Henry, and Leah standing at the edge of the circle staring. But what was really weird was that the voice which had told them to stop was familiar. Lucas?

THIRTY ONE

Claire raced past her niece at the sound of Lucas's voice. What was he doing out in the woods at this hour? When she got to the spot beside Maya, her breath froze in her chest.

Lucas had a gun in his hand waving it in an arc aimed at each of them in turn! Beside him was a shovel and a deep hole. But it was the body laying beside him that made her jerk back.

A young woman in a red hoodie, her blond hair splayed across the grass lay there. Her eyes were open in a face that held the gray pallor of death.

"Lucas! What?" Her heart raced in her chest seeing the gun in his hand and the wild, desperate look in his eyes. She pulled Maya in behind her.

"Drop the gun, Lucas!" Jake stepped forward and Lucas aimed it at him.

"Don't come any closer or I'll shoot!" Lucas cocked the trigger. The snap was like a knife to her gut. He had killed the young woman. It was the same woman she'd seen peering in the door. Skylar. Oh my God. He'd killed that woman, and he wouldn't hesitate to kill any of them.

Movement at the far side of the clearing caught her eye. The old lady? Mrs. Kovac stepped out from the trees. Her arms were raised and the forefinger of each hand crossed each other as she advanced. She mumbled words in a low voice while her narrow eyes were riveted to Lucas.

Lucas must have sensed her or heard her murmuring because he turned slightly, now aiming the gun at her.

He jerked and fell to the side before the thunderclap of the gunshot registered in her ears. A red hole flared in his temple, spattering blood on the grass beside him when he landed. Claire gasped. It had happened so quickly!

Jake stepped forward, the gun still smoking in his outstretched hand before him.

"Oh my God! Lucas was going to kill us!" She could only stare as Jake approached the downed man slowly, with the gun still aimed at him.

Maya clasped Claire's waist, openly crying into her chest. "Aunt Claire! He killed Skylar! He was going to kill us!"

Henry added, "Thank God your uncle was here."

"And Mrs. Kovac." Ashley walked like she was in a trance over to the old woman. The old crone stood stock-still, muttering in some foreign language, staring at Lucas. "Mrs. Kovac?"

She watched Jake rise from where he had squatted to check for a pulse, slipping his gun back into his jacket.

He looked over at Claire and shook his head slowly, "This was your boyfriend? This is Lucas? And you had him around my *nieces*?"

Tears rolled down her cheeks and it was hard to find her voice, "I didn't know! Oh my God! I told him everything last night on the phone!"

Preston had moved over to the girl's body and he touched her cheek with his fingertips. Henry and Mason joined him looking at her while Leah and Ashley stood next to the old woman. All of this was going on but for Claire it barely registered in her brain. She clung to Maya, rubbing the girl's back and murmuring, "I'm sorry," over and over again.

Sorry for bringing such a monster anywhere near them. Sorry for the poor girl he'd murdered. Sorry she'd ever met him. Sorry... She looked over at Jake watching him speak on his cell phone, calling this in to his office.

Sorry that they had split up. But there was no going back.

THIRTY TWO

Ashley's feet moved automatically walking over to the old woman. Her mind had shut down when Lucas had stood there with a gun in his hands threatening to kill them. He'd already killed poor Skylar. Her face still held the marks where he'd beaten and strangled her. But Lucas was gone now. Thanks to the old woman showing up.

And for Uncle Jake.

Leah walked with her and reached to touch the old woman's arm. "Mrs. Kovac?"

The old woman's eyes were dark, shiny like the eyes of a crow, staring first at Leah and then turning to Ashley. Her skin was like worn leather, tanned and creased with lines. Wisps of white hair poked from under a gray scarf, and her fingers were claws when she gripped Ashley's shoulder. "I tried to warn you."

Ashley's eyes welled with tears. "Yes. I know that now."

"How did you know?" Leah was crying as well but managed to get the words out.

"Later. It is not finished." The old woman stepped away from them and went over to the girl's body, dropping down on her knees next to Preston.

Ashley watched her scoop a handful of earth and roll in into her fingers. She placed her index finger on the Skylar's forehead leaving a streak of dirt there.

"Hey! Don't touch her! This is a crime scene."

But she ignored Jake's words and her fingers touched the girl's chest, leaving a smudge in the red sweater over the girl's heart. All the while she muttered an incantation.

She looked over at Maya and then turned to Preston, touching his forehead and saying more words. When she pushed at the earth trying to get up, Ashley and Leah bent to help her rise. Again, her bony finger rose to touch first Leah and then Ashley's forehead.

Her head jerked to the side where Maya stood with Aunt Claire. Slowly they made their way over so that she could repeat the ritual with her sister.

Ashley's eyes went wider, when her hand rose again to touch her aunt's face. The old lady smiled at Claire. "You know what you must do now. It has followed you since you were a teenager. It must be destroyed."

Ashley knew without being told what she was referring to.

The Ouija board.

Henry came over. "What about me and my brother? We were there too. Don't we get the blessing or whatever it is you did to them?"

She sniggered and then smiled showing more than a few gaps in her teeth. Her hand rose to tap his forehead and she looked over at Mason.

He shook his head. "I'm good. I don't need that, whatever it is."

She crooked her finger beckoning him closer. He huffed a sigh and at a snail's pace came over to stand before her. His eyes closed as her hand rose to touch him as well.

Ashley looked over and tried to see past her uncle to where Lucas lay on the ground. The man who'd almost killed them. Even her aunt who had cared for him didn't go near him to weep over his death.

She thought of the Ouija board and how Skylar had taken over from their contact with their parents. If she hadn't, would Lucas have gotten away with killing her? She turned to Maya and then pulled her into her arms.

They'd never know the answer to that question. She was just glad it was over.

THIRTY THREE

Late August

Ashley looked up at the sky as she floated in the water. The taunts and laughter from the raft closer to shore was muted and only the sound of her breathing and heartbeat filled her ears. She closed her eyes enjoying the sun's warmth on her face while her body was cooled by the lake. It was hard to believe that the summer was practically over and that she'd be a sophomore at Saranac High.

Something bounced off her head and she jerked up in the water, looking toward the raft. A red and white beach ball floated near her while Maya and Henry laughed.

Maya yelled to her, "Hey! Aunt Claire has lunch ready. You looked like you were almost asleep out there."

Preston smiled. "I told them not to do that. But you know Henry." He spun around and raced at Henry, the two of them falling off the raft into the water with a cannonball jump.

She swam lazily toward them watching her sister peer into the water after them. One good thing about that whole nightmare experience had been Preston's speech. Whatever had happened, he no longer stuttered. And Maya now seemed to favor him above Henry. She smiled. You could only take so much of a constant smart-ass.

Leah was on the shore with Mason, the two of them helping Aunt Claire with the BBQ and lunch. She looked over when Henry popped up next to her. "Did she bring that awful soup, do you think? Who makes a soup out of cabbage? And it's red. Yuck."

Ashley splashed a handful of water at him. "It's borsch. She grows her own cabbage and you'll have some to be polite."

The old lady came out of the back door ahead of her aunt. Even though it was almost eighty degrees she wore a sweater and long skirt. She'd ditched the headscarf though and her white hair was in a long braid wound around her head. Since she'd been a regular visitor at their house, it was like years had fallen from her stooped shoulders. And her English had improved. Mrs. Kovac looked over the water and waved to Ashley before Leah herded her into the chair she'd gotten out for her.

Ashley looked at the driveway. Still no sign of Jake and he'd promised her he'd come out. Her feet bumped into the sandy bottom and she stood up, turning her head to squeeze the water from her ponytail.

Mason saw her and then walked over with a towel in his outstretched hand. "Here. You're getting prune fingers, you've been in the water so long."

She winked at him and then went up on her tiptoes to kiss his cheek. "You just missed me is all."

As she walked beside him, she glanced at her Aunt Claire. She was much quieter these days. She'd also cut back on her hours at the office. She was even talking about going back to school and getting her accountant's license. Carol thought she could get her a job at the casino, although she wasn't keen. Probably because of the association of the casino and Lucas.

She'd been so wrong about that guy. Uncle Jake had gotten the whole story and told them. Lucas wasn't an investment guy. He was into human trafficking and running a prostitute ring. His father had been pressuring him about getting married to give him better cover for his illegal activities. Just Aunt Claire's luck that he'd latched onto her.

Aunt Claire also said that she was in the process of breaking up with him when this whole episode began. Maya believed her, but Ashley was dubious. Until Carol told her the same thing, and showed the text messages between her and Aunt Claire discussing it. Carol said she was going to make a point of visiting Syracuse and showing the messages on her phone to Jake.

And she did.

Ashley's reverie ended when Maya and her two sidekicks raced by them, diving into the bowl of potato chips on the picnic table.

Leah turned to her brother. "Preston! You guys! Save some for the rest of us." She snatched the bowl from in front of them and took it over to the old lady offering her some.

Aunt Claire looked over at Ashley, sharing a look. Ever since that awful day, Leah had taken it upon herself to be a self-appointed protégé of the old woman. It drove her mother crazy which was half the reason she did it. Leah was no longer cowering to her mother's fanaticism. And she had an ally in Preston. The old lady, for her part, didn't mind Leah's attention, especially when it came to weeding her garden.

Ashley looked up at the sound of her uncle's voice. He carried a bottle of wine and a bunch of flowers in his arms. Holy cow! She'd told him to show up but she never expected him to go all out. He was even freshly shaved and wearing a golf shirt that looked brand new, from the crease in the sleeves.

"Hey girls! Guys." He nodded over at the old lady and with a flourish he handed the flowers to her. "*Ma bucur sa te vad, Margrit.*"

"*Vraijitor*!" But her cheeks colored as she took them from him. "*Multumiri.*" She looked over at Claire. "I called him a charmer." She looked back at Jake. "These should be for her."

He handed the bottle of wine to Claire. "No. This is her

favorite as I recall."

Claire took the bottle from him and then looped her arm around his neck pulling him down to kiss his lips.

Ashley blinked a few times and looked over at Maya. There was hope for these two yet. How many times had they talked on the phone behind hers and Maya's back?

The steaks on the BBQ weren't the only thing cooking.

Jake took Claire's hand in his and smiled down at her. He turned to Ashley and Maya. "We've got an announcement to make. We're getting married."

"Again! Can you believe it?" Claire grinned from ear to ear and held out her hand for them to see the ring on her finger.

So it wasn't just phone calls. That explained Claire being away for the last two weekends on "courses." Ashley and Maya raced over to them and hugged each of them in turn.

"I'm so happy that you're getting back together!" Ashley felt like her chest would explode.

Jake pulled back looking at them. "I've quit my job but I've got a pretty good line on a position at the sheriff's office here."

Maya leapt into his arms. "Oh my God! That's great!"

Ashley looked over at the movement beside the house and waved seeing Carol arriving.

Carol watched Jake as she sauntered over. "What's going on?" She stopped short and her hand flew to her mouth. "Oh my God! You guys are getting back together?"

It became a flurry of hugs and gushing between Carol and Claire. Ashley turned to her sister. "I think Mom and Dad would be happy about this."

Maya's smile was wistful. "But we'll have to trust in that. There's no way I'm ever using a Ouija board again."

THE END

AUTHOR'S NOTE

I hope you enjoyed 'A Grave Conjuring'; I found writing it to be deeply rewarding. Yes, as I type these words, I already miss Henry's wise-cracking too!

A Grave Conjuring is the second book I wrote in this series. You will meet new characters; and characters from previous books often times appear. In each tale of 'The Haunted Ones', I chronicle ordinary people coping with unspeakable evil from the other side.

In the book publishing business, honest reviews are more important than ever; and that's true for the big, famous writers as well as little ol' me. I deeply appreciate everyone who takes the time to let others know what they think of my work.

Michelle Dorey

ABOUT MICHELLE DOREY

A multiple bestselling author, Michelle Dorey has written more than a dozen spine-chilling novels featuring ghosts, haunted houses and the supernatural.

A voracious reader of the masters like Stephen King and Dean Koontz, her debut novel was inspired by attending a Ghost Walk in the enigmatic city of Kingston, Ontario, Canada. Crawley House was inspired by a true tale of a family's nightmare, living in a Victorian era home.

"Expect the supernatural when the bedrock of a city is limestone. When this ancient rock is surrounded on three sides by water as my home town is... well, you have the perfect setting for eerie events--which of course is my cup of tea."

Wife and mother, Michelle is also a dog lover, human to Suki and Ruby. She loves them dearly, but for the last eight years on walks, they absolutely refuse to enter grounds of a beautiful historic cemetery near her home.

Michelle has written two complete series, The Hauntings Of Kingston and The Mystical Veil. She's currently at work on her latest, The Haunted Ones--set in upper New York State.

OTHER WORKS
BY
MICHELLE DOREY

THE HAUNTINGS OF KINGSTON SERIES

The city of Kingston is enigmatic; where the line between this world and the next becomes quite hazy. A ghostly series inspired by this historic and sometimes mysterious place. Each novel is a stand alone:

Crawley House
The Haunted Inn
The Ghosts Of Centre Street
The Haunting Of Larkspur Farm
The Ghosts Of Hanson House

THE MYSTICAL VEIL

Twenty four year old trust fund brat Keira Swanson finds out that her family has secrets. Secrets of the dead…

Legacy
Heritage
Forsaken
Ascendant

PARANORMAL SUSPENSE

The Haunted Ones

Ordinary people confront malevolent spirits in each of these eerie tales…

The Haunted Hideout
A Grave Conjuring
Haunted By The Succubus
The Haunted Gathering
The Haunted Reckoning
Graveyard Shift

SPECIAL BONUS:

The first two chapters of

The Haunted Gathering

Another Epidode of The Haunted Ones!

ABOUT THE HAUNTED GATHERING

On their annual girls' weekend three friends gather for a macabre reunion in this chilling tale of ghosts, hauntings and the occult.

Dara died almost a year ago, and her three closest surviving friends gather in accordance with her last wishes at Gabbinger's Reach—a once abandoned resort she planned on restoring to opulence.

The derelict property has been decaying for decades. Cindy the career woman thinks this is stupid. Melanie, the flighty one is fascinated. Becky, now a therapist is curious—why would Dara want them here?

They're enticed to stay by Dara's Last Will and Testament. Each of them are promised riches, all they need to do is remain here for two nights.

When darkness descends on the first evening, they laugh off the sudden appearance of small gifts. They're only a little startled by things crashing around in the kitchen. Someone's trying to spook them; big freaking deal—Cindy brought a gun!

Their bravado is tested when they begin to uncover long

held secrets. Secrets about each another, secrets about Dara, and long hidden secrets about the evil that infests the very walls of this place. Hungry evil relishing fresh victims.

At the same time their bonds of friendship are at the breaking point, the ravenous beast descends in a mighty fury. In a night of terror, they know they'll never be the same. If they survive.

Dara didn't.

The Haunted Gathering

MICHELLE DOREY

The Haunted Ones 4

ONE

Rebecca finished typing the last entry into Bobbi Penstock's file. It had been a longer day than usual, cramming her schedule to clear up some time in September for the annual get-together. She clicked the mouse bringing up her personal email.

When Dara's email popped up, she smiled. *Finally* there'd be some details of where they'd meet. Trust Dara to leave everything to the last minute, just like in college. Some things never changed.

To: Becky, Melanie, Cindy

Date: Monday, June 28 at 10:43 PM

Subject: Our 7th Annual Reunion Bash

Hi ladies,

SEVEN years since Caltech! What the hell? Even crazier is the fact that I actually miss that place...sometimes.

I know you're on the edge of your seats waiting for details of our get-together (or as Melanie calls it "the gathering") At least I hope you are sitting down because...

I've got SUPER fantastic plans for our reunion this year.

I BOUGHT A FREAKING RESORT!

That's right. Dara Zuckerman is now the official owner of Gabbinger's Reach, in the Catskill Mountains.

And before you suggest I sign up for a few sessions of psycho-therapy with you, Becky, it was the deal of a lifetime. Too good to pass up! Rock-bottom sticker price.

I don't know how much you know about the Borsch belt in the Catskills, but in its heyday (1950s and 60s) it was THE place for rich New York Jewish folks to get away from the heat of the city to relax. I'm not going to go into the anti-Semitism that was rampant during that time in NYC, (which, thank God has changed), but the popularity of the area fell off during the 70s and 80s.

Like other resorts, Gabbinger's has been abandoned for DECADES! Sure, it needs work and MONEY, of which I've got tons. Thanks Daddy, for that at least. (sigh)

You're going to love it, Melanie, with the scenic mountains and the lake practically at our front door. Who knows with these buff construction guys, you may even finally get a boyfriend. Got to put yourself out there a bit, Mel. Put down the crystals, tarot cards and books and join the living instead of the dead. You might like it. (Teasing of course. You know I love you just the way you are.)

Don't worry about how rustic and primitive it is, Cindy. By SEPTEMBER, our accommodations will be TOTALLY revamped with every convenience you'd ever want.

(After what happened in Chicago, I owe you that much at least, although I know I was right doing it. All forgiven? If not, we can count on Becky to "therapy" us, just like back in the good old days sharing that house on campus. Remember the ice-cream incident? That could have gotten real ugly if not for Becky.)

Becky, give my regards to Hank. He's gonna have to cook for himself while you're gone but Boo Hoo. LOL

I know this is a far stretch from the glitzy Vegas trip, Cindy. Or traipsing over Mayan Ruins, Melanie...or even the seaside resort in Rockport, Becky... BUT it's my turn to choose the venue this year.

My turn, my resort. So there. Suck it up, Buttercups.

Besides which, I'm dying to show it to you, my oldest and dearest friends! Well...maybe not as it is today but what I'm going to DO with it!

Did I mention that the area is under consideration by the state for more casino expansion? That's where the REAL money is. Well that's one avenue that makes this worthwhile, but I've got some other ideas too. How about an Adults Only Spa? I don't care as long as they have full pockets for me to plunder. Hopefully you'll come up with more ideas!

I've had a crew up there for a month working. There's a section of the resort that's once more habitable for us. Don't worry, I'm going there tomorrow to crack the whip and make sure of it.

I'm attaching a few pics of the area as well as a map. Not sure the Google Car ever made it this far into the boonies.

Besties forever,

Dara

Rebecca sank back in the leather chair and exhaled slowly. Dara bought a resort in the Catskills? With the death of her father last year she now had total control of the estate, so why not? Still, maybe she was biting off more than she could chew. Delayed grief reaction? Trying hard to relive her father's dreams? But she had made a tidy profit when she'd sold that art gallery two years ago.

The intercom on her desk buzzed bringing her out of the reverie. "Yes?"

"Your eleven o'clock is here. Shall I send him in?" Gloria's low voice let her know that Jason Knox was probably perched on the edge of the chair in the waiting room. No doubt his knee was twitching, looking forward to unloading the slights and injustices he'd suffered at the hands of his domineering mother the past week. No matter that he was thirty-four and still living under his parents' roof with zero job prospects.

"Give me five, Gloria. I'm just finishing up an article." No need to tell her receptionist she was still pondering Dara's email.

What was that *Chicago* thing all about? Something happened there between Dara and Cindy? Maybe she'd give Cindy a call later to get the dirt. Probably Dara had done something thoughtless. Tact and diplomacy weren't her strong suits, whereas Cindy was people-smart. She had to be to make it in that cutthroat business.

Rebecca turned slightly to gaze out the window at the expanse of chrome and mirrored buildings. If she leaned closer there was even a partial view of the Olympic Mountains, maybe if it wasn't hazy and overcast. Prime office space in downtown Seattle. Not bad for a kid who grew up in neighboring Tacoma. Like Melanie and Cindy, she'd had to work two jobs in the summer to pay for tuition. Even so, she was still paying off her student loans.

Dara. How they'd ever hooked up with a trust-fund kid and became friends was still a wonder. But to give Dara credit, she *was* fun to hang with. There was never a dull moment with her antics. Maybe she'd finally found her place in life with this abandoned resort, breathing life into it.

She pushed the button on her desk signaling that she was ready for Jason Knox. She'd answer the email after his session.

Never knowing that by that time, Dara would be dead.

TWO

That September...

"You didn't make her *funeral,* Cindy. This is the least that you can do!" Holding the phone in a death grip, Rebecca gritted her teeth so hard they clicked. It was bad enough that Cindy refused to tell her about the altercation she'd had with Dara in Chicago, but here she was trying to dodge the last request that Dara would ever make!

"Come on, Beck! Don't try to guilt me into going. As for the funeral, I was in *Australia*, for Pete's sake! Even if I decided to risk losing our biggest client and come back I still couldn't have made it in time." The exasperation in Cindy's voice bordered on being whiny.

"Look. All I'm saying is that it's the last thing we'll ever get to do for Dara. And what about Melanie? You know how close to Dara she is...or rather was. This will totally devastate her if we all don't show up at this Gabbinger's place. *She* needs our support if nothing else." Rebecca's eyes narrowed. Whatever had happened between Cindy and Dara had to be pretty rough if she was so willing to skip out on the dead woman's last request.

Cindy's tone softened, "Poor Mel. But it's just so morbid. I mean Dara drowned there. And that thing in her will is creepy as hell. Who makes a will before they're even thirty, anyway?"

"I know. I wondered about that too. Was she depressed? Why would she go swimming at night, *alone*?" It wasn't the first time that she wondered if Dara had been suicidal. But she hadn't talked to Dara in months. Not something she was proud of, but people have their own lives. They get busy.

"That was so *Dara*. Invincible. She paid the ultimate price for her recklessness." There was silence for a few beats, both of them picturing their friend. "Have you spoken to Melanie? I mean since the funeral."

"I texted her a few times, and when she didn't answer I finally called. She's adamant that we all go there, to honor Dara's wishes. She... Well, you'll see for yourself anyway, but...she's gotten even more obsessed with this spiritualism shit."

"Of course she has. She'll never change." Cindy's tone went from wistful to annoyed in the next breath. "That letter we all got from her lawyer...It wouldn't have killed him to give us more information to go on. Just be at Gabbinger's September twenty-first at four p.m. to honor Dara's last wishes. And we have to stay the weekend?"

Becky's voice hitched when she spoke. "Of course you know that Dara's birthday is September twenty-second . She would have been twenty-eight. Way too young to die."

"You think she left us anything in the will?"

"Cindy! Is that all you're—"

"NO!" Her voice became softer after Becky's chastisement. "Just wondering is all. None of us need it. Well...maybe Mel could use it. But money was never Melanie's thing, right? Give her a book about goblins and poltergeists, and she's lost in her own world."

"She's not as strong as the rest of us, Cindy. That sort of stuff is her crutch--escaping into make-believe. That way she doesn't have to risk real relationships. I don't think she's made any friends since us back in university. She needs us, Cindy. Say you'll come. It's only forty-eight hours. Surely you can put your career on hold for that long."

A long sigh followed, and Becky's head rose higher. When Cindy mumbled a soft, "I guess," her eyes closed with relief.

She decided to press ahead before Cindy had a chance to change her mind. "My flight arrives in Newark at one ten. Mel's getting there at noon. I've booked a car for us. You're welcome to drive with us."

"How far is it from the airport?" Cindy's voice drooped with resignation.

"Two hours. Seriously, we might even manage to have fun, you know. I'm bringing wine. We can count on Mel for weed. We'll celebrate Dara's birthday as if she were there." Becky tried to sound upbeat, barely pulling it off. Yes. Cindy was right. This was downright weirdly morbid.

Still, it would be good to see Mel and Cindy. But the reunion bash with just the three of them, where Dara had actually died, was going to be sad.

To say the least. Partying at the spot where one of your best friends died? She shuddered inwardly.

"Fine. I'll book the flight and see you tomorrow. This place better have a damn bathroom! I'm not using some outhouse or something. And that lawyer, Anthony Wilson, better have it well stocked with food and drink."

"Thanks, Cindy. I also want to know what went down with you and Dara in Chicago."

"Don't push your luck, Becky." This was followed by a click.

Made in the USA
Monee, IL
15 June 2021

71366273R10115